A Frosty Mug of Murder

by

Constance Barker

Sign up for Constance Barker's New Releases
Newsletter

Chapter One

"I'll be there in just a sec." I had to yell so she could hear me all the way downstairs. It was only quarter past ten and I could hear Dixie was early for work. My father and I live above the town pub and I was ready to get to work anyway. After taking one last sip of my coffee, I tied my wavy, red hair up into a pony tail, and left to join her. She greeted me when I was half way down the stairs.

"Ginger, look at this! This is plain weird now!" Dixie blew past Good Morning I guess to get to the complaining. Not really unusual for her. But she had a point. I could see the pickled egg jar was once again smashed on the floor behind the bar.

"Son of a ... I took it off the counter last night and put it in the condiments cabinet. Behind closed doors!" I knew I did. My theory was that one of Donna's many cats was sneaking into the bar at night and knocking the big, lidded jar over. But a cat would not be able to get into that cabinet.

Dixie hovered her hands over the large pool of juice, sprinkled with broken glass and pickled eggs, to emphasize the size of the puddle. "Well it did. It fell over, knocked the cabinet door open, and crashed on the floor. Look at this mess. It even got under the wet sink. I don't like having my bar area trashed."

It always made a mess and smelled awful. This was getting out of hand and the eight broken jars cost me a fortune. Not only did I have to replace the jar, all the pickled eggs needed to be restocked too. Running a pub is hard work and making a profit is almost impossible. I know when something is costing us too much. And the broken pickled egg jars were burning money. "You know what Dixie, I'm not replacing it this time."

"Come on, Ginger. Guardrail is going to be upset if you don't restock his favorite. He loves those pickled eggs. And he's one of your best customers."

"Dixie, are you sweet on that big lug?" She tended bar here for thirty years, so I know her well. She's not afraid to tell it like it is and rarely shows sympathy or concern, especially when she is on her hands and knees in pickle juice and broken glass.

Dixie snorted. "You can't be serious! No! He tips real good, especially when he drinks a little. And he drinks more when he is eating these nasty eggs."

I eyed her sideways, knowing better. I could swear she actually blushed a little but it was hard to see her clearly behind the bar.

Guardrail's real name was Brian, but no one called him that, and he runs a motorcycle shop not far from my pub. To look at him, he is a big, Harley riding brute. But looks can be deceiving and I know that he would give you the shirt off his back if you needed it. I'm not certain, but I think he may have even done Dixie a favor or two over the years.

"Hang on. I'll give you a hand. Let me get the grill on to heat up for the lunch crowd and get an apron." I grabbed a dirty apron, because I learned from the past seven times it was impossible to clean up this mess and not get pickle juice all over you.

Dixie threw the over soaked rag down on the ground in disgust. "Thanks, but I got it. You get the kitchen going. I know we got lunch to take care of, and after that, the food for Stitch N Bitch night needs to be prepared. And by the way, Bones isn't here yet."

Carl and Bessie Houston owned Sew Fabric, the local yarn and fabric store. Every Tuesday night they sponsored a get together at The Grumpy Chicken for people to share sewing, knitting, crocheting, and any other crafting tips. There was no real sales pitch, but Carl and Bessie sometimes used the occasion to push projects centered around some new product they now carried. Bless their souls, they tried hard to make make it a party like atmosphere, but it always turned into more of a session for locals to complain and spread gossip. Juicy tidbits were traded far more than sewing tips, so Dixie and I called it Stitch N Bitch instead of Tuesday night.

This may be a good time to mention that The Grumpy Chicken is an Irish pub in Potter's Mill, Georgia, about forty-five minutes from Savannah. It's a small town, and as cliche as it is, we just had our first traffic light installed. And I'm not kidding, but no one here seems to know how to use it right, or maybe they all just ignore it. Like I said, we are a tiny spot on the map.

Gossip is a big deal in a small place like ours, so Stitch N Bitch is a not-to-miss event and normally well attended. It's good for my business and we sell a fair amount of drinks and food. Tonight, we're doing Buffalo wings and prepping enough chicken ahead of time for thirty or so people is a ton of work. But first, we have to get through the lunch rush.

In a lick, customers were ordering sandwiches and drinks, and the early lunch rush was on. However, Bones, our busboy, who also helps with the cooking, was still missing. His real name is Jeff Lewis, and like most nineteen year old boys, he has a lot to learn about life. He is decent looking and tall, but skinny. And I mean thin, thinner than a sheet of phyllo dough. That's how he got his nickname, all bones and no meat.

Finally, just before noon when I had started half of the lunch orders on the grill, he tried slinking into the kitchen. I stopped him short. "Bones! Where have you been, we got lunch to serve and after that we need to rearrange the dining room. And the food order for Stitch N Bitch has to be prepped. Especially all the wings."

Bones replied in a soft voice. "I had to move again. My room mate threw me out."

"You mean your girl friend of the week? Well that's not news, and not my problem, I need you here on time."

"I'm sorry Boss. I won't be late again." Bones hung his head as he talked. He liked this job and wanted to keep it. Why, I'm not sure. He seemed nonchalant about his work at times, but was good at it when he focused. He sheepishly added, "I'll make it up to ya, Boss, promise."

"Well, get your apron on and get started. Hit the grill, I'll get the tables."

With my full team present, we easily handled the early lunch crowd, even after starting our day with a pickled egg disaster and Bones showing up late.

I tended to a table occupied by Piper and Ida. "How was everything today?"

"Fine, despite having an amateur like you cook my chicken breast." Piper knew I was on the grill till Bones showed. I was best friends with Piper Freeman in high school. But she left town for college after we graduated. And after college she took a journalist's job at a big paper in Atlanta, so she was gone for a few years. Eventually, she got fed up with the big city and office politics and returned to Potter's Mill. I'm glad to have her back and we are best friends again. By the way, she now owns and prints her own paper, The Potter's Mill Oracle. Not sure what oracle we have here, I think Piper just fixates on some words and has to use them.

I folded my arms. "Thanks, I think. I know how to use a grill, ya know."

"Oh, I'm just having fun with you. Lighten up. Hey Ginger, Dixie told me you had another egg jar broken last night." Piper used her napkin to wipe some Dijon mustard from the grilled chicken sandwich off her lips while she spoke.

"Yeah, that makes eight pickled egg jars killed in the line of duty at The Grumpy Chicken." I held up eight fingers to emphasize the number.

"You should have a wall of stars to commemorate them." Piper laughed at her own joke. "Hey, y'all think it's that chicken ghost thing that haunts this place. Has to be."

I snapped back, "No! It's one of Donna Holland's cats. She has so many of them and they're always getting into something. Let's not exaggerate."

Ida broke her silence. "I don't know. I've heard a lot of stories about the ghoulish hen clucking and making noises in here at night. And don't forget, the bird that haunts this place gave it the name Grumpy Chicken."

"Stop Ida! We don't need you whipping up people to tell more false stories. Me and Dad argue all the time about whether that naming story is actually true." But I knew Ida was right. This pub has been in my family for one hundred and fifty years and it was originally named after a chicken that supposedly haunts the place. The Grumpy Chicken has been handed down through generations, along with the name and the ghost stories. I tried to downplay the ghost stories, they spooked some of our regulars and I was afraid it could hurt business.

My father, Tom O'Mallory, now owns the place, but I'm the one who has to run the daily business. My dad is out of town now, getting some much needed medical attention for a cough he can't seem to shake. So lucky me, I'm alone and running everything right now.

Digger, the local grave-digger, came through the front door and headed for the bar.

Dixie greeted him. "You here for the remains of jar number eight? It died a horrible death last night and it is not a pretty thing to see."

Digger sighed in response, smiled, and then leaned on the bar. "Ha, Ha, Ha, Dixie. You might try teasing me with something a little different than grave-digger humor. Is my take out order ready?" He scanned the counter in back of Dixie. "Wait, the jar is really gone, so it took a dive last night?"

Dixie chuckled. "Yep. Right in the middle of bar floor. Splat. I spent my first hour here this morning cleaning it up."

"Dang, that chicken really is grumpy. I can see

where it would hate having pickled eggs around, though. Ya know, being a chicken and all."

Dixie tilted her head back. "That's kind of obvious too, Einstein. Tell ya what, you get more original with your jokes, and so will I."

"Deal! I'll work on writing new jokes if you do. Ya know, this jar thing is getting to the point I think we should start a pool. One of those guess how long the next jar … "

Dixie interrupted. "No can do. Ginger says she's not replacing it."

Digger snorted. "Who's going to tell Guardrail."

Back at the table I was tending, Ida popped up in her seat. "Hey, Ginger, I got an idea. You're so low tech here, lets bring you into the twenty-first century. I can set up a web cam, record the egg jar overnight and see if you're right about a cat knocking it over." Ida Bell was smart. She could do anything with a computer, and it was a miracle she never got into trouble because if she wanted something, she wasn't afraid to do a little hacking to get it.

"It's a pub Ida, we serve drinks and food, not electronics. But ya know what, let's do it. I am going to show y'all, it's those pesky cats. By the way, it won't cost me anything, right?" I was a little too sure of myself about the cats, but hey, I knew I was right.

"No, silly. I'm your friend and want to help! It won't cost you a penny." Ida seemed too sweet today. She could be a pill at times, well actually most of the time. What was she up to?

And as if on cue, a black cat wandered through the dining area. I knew the cat. It was Gypsy, and you may have guessed, it belonged to Donna. This particular cat could be a little mean and didn't like people. Except for one. For some reason the animal seemed to tolerate me.

"See, I wouldn't be surprised to see it was Gypsy here that's knocking over stuff." I picked up the cat and could feel it purring.

Dixie chimed in from behind the bar. "You need to get that cat out of here. An inspector won't like seeing an animal in here."

She was right. But we still had to finish lunch and get ready for Stitch N Bitch. "I can't leave, we have too much to do."

"Oh no, that cat won't let anyone else touch it. You bring it back to Donna's place, and come right on back. It's not far and won't take long. I'll hold down things just fine while you're gone." Dixie believed in some of the ghost stories, I knew, and I realized she perceived a black cat in the pub as bad luck. She wanted the feline gone, now.

"Bones, help Dixie close out lunch and get set for tonight. I need to bring one of Donna's nomads home." I usually didn't yell through the service window, but I wasn't going to carry the cat into the kitchen.

"What's a nomad? Shoot, you're leaving because you're still mad at me for being late, aren't ya Boss?" Bones flipped a few burgers and dropped some more fries into hot oil while he spoke. I have to admit, he could work when he wanted to.

I added, "No. Don't be so sensitive, or we'll have to change your name to Baby."

"That might be confusing, Boss, that's what I call my girlfriends. We can't both be called Baby." I saw him smiling at me through the order window.

I smacked my forehead. "I can't believe I am having this conversation! I'm taking the cat home. See y'all. Will be right back."

I was actually grateful to Gypsy for getting me outside in some fresh air. Bones had the grill under control, and while Dixie usually tended bar, she could wait and bus tables too when she had to. The pub would be just fine for a few minutes without me.

I made it to Donna Holland's house fast enough. It's located about four blocks from The Grumpy Chicken and hard to miss. The Holland's own an old home, and by far it's the largest house in Potter's Mill. Donna had a number of additions made to the place, and it is hard to describe. Well it was plain weird, there I said it. But even with the bizarre add-ons, the original large round tower, steep roofs, and slate shingles still dominate the front facade enough to let you know this was originally a Victorian by design.

The place is well kept, even with all the cats. At least a dozen ran off as I carried Gypsy up the front walk, but they moved too fast for me to identify them all. However, I did spot Snowball run across the lawn and Harry Potter jumped up and ran off when I turned up the front walk. I wasn't sure if Harry ran from me or Gypsy. Tigger and Stewy were more brave, staying in their prized spots on the porch rail. I didn't really know these two cats, so I just called them what seemed to make sense.

I slowly climbed the porch stairs making my way to the front door. I don't know why, but the big round tower on one corner of the structure and the large, dark front door made the house look like the bad place in a horror movie. And I was carrying a black cat, what was I doing? I briefly thought about dropping the cat and running off. For some reason I felt apprehensive. But I forced myself to stop being silly and approached the front door. Thank goodness it was light out.

I used the fancy knocker to announce my presence at the front door. I didn't want to break the pretty brass striker, so I gently tapped – clank, clank. But no one responded. I then banged on the door a little harder with my hand, causing the door to crack open slightly. I stuck my head in for a quick peek. "Hello.

Anyone home?" Then I saw it, and unfortunately someone was home, lying strangely still on the floor. All I could see was the lower half of a single leg. The leg was nicely dressed in a lace stocking with a high-heeled shoe laying on its side next to the foot. I instantly knew this was going to be a strange day indeed.

Chapter Two

I opened the door slowly and pushed into the entrance, just a little. Then I saw Donna Holland lying on her back, hands at her neck and eyes open, staring blankly at the ceiling. Her legs were bent at odd angles and both of her high-heeled shoes sat nearby, apparently falling off during a scuffle. She looked dead. One of her cats didn't seem to notice the horrific scene and sniffed an empty shoe lying on its side, then navigated around the still body and sauntered out of the room.

I moved toward her, slowly, taking care not to disturb a thing. Especially the cats, they were everywhere and I almost stepped on Brandy. I made it to Donna and knelt by her side. I could see her chest was still; she wasn't breathing. Worse, I cautiously touched the side of her neck and couldn't find a pulse. Cher took the occasion to rub against me and I could hear her purring as I took out my cell phone to call the police. Deputy Mae Owens answered. "Mae, its Ginger."

"Oh! Hi honey, how are you doing?"

"Aunt Mae, listen. I'm at Donna Holland's place and I just found her on the floor. I think she's dead. You should get out here … Cher, shoo!"

"What? … Who are you talking too? … Ginger, listen carefully. Don't touch anything and wait outside. I'll be right over."

"Send an ambulance too. I pretty sure she's dead, but you know, I'm not a doctor."

"Sure, sweetie, I'll be there in a few minutes. Don't touch a thing and get out of there, that may be a crime scene now. I'm coming right now." And Mae hung up.

I clicked my phone off and looked around. Donna Holland was young and in good health. Mae said it may be a crime scene, and it was plausible that someone murdered Donna. I couldn't help but wonder what had happened, so I took did a quick once over of the scene.

Donna's hair was elaborately done up in an Elizabeth Hurley knock off and she wore a pretty dress as if prepared for a night out. A little too formal for this early in the day if you asked me.

Instead of a necklace, a cord was wrapped around

her throat. I also detected weird purple dots on her neck and all around her ears. Her hands rested under her chin, in an apparent attempt to stop someone from choking her and remove the cord that was wrapped around her neck.

I scanned the room from my knees. This space was originally a large study, but Donna now used it as a family room. A desk sat proudly off to one side with a full bookcase behind it, almost as if claiming squatter rights from the original study.

Along another wall, a sofa and coffee table provided a nice place to sit and talk, or watch the large screen television directly across from the formal seating area. Far from formal, two bean bag chairs provided the only other seating and were placed right in front of the television; one had a wireless video game controller in the dent where someone had been sitting.

The center of the hardwood floor was covered by a fine Persian rug, but the beautiful light oak showed all around the perimeter of the room. I could see faint scuffs in the freshly vacuumed surface that looked like feet dragging across the fibers of the carpet.

Lighting came from a small chandelier in the center of the ceiling and from expensive looking floor lamps on either side of the sofa, but one of the floor standing lamps laid on its side. The only other source of light was from a banker's lamp on the desk, but it laid on the floor, broken.

And, last but not least, there were two well occupied cat towers stuffed into a couple of the room's corners. I couldn't believe how many cats those things held. Then I noticed one of the towers sat at an odd angle, and would have fallen if the wall corner had not propped it up. That is also when I saw Trixie, she was laying just next to the leaning tower, licking a hind leg. She seemed to have hurt the limb.

In spite of all the cats, I detected the smell of a cheap floral perfume, so I bent closer to Donna's head. She wore an expensive perfume that smelled wonderful. But it was not the smell lingering in the room air.

Then I saw pearls strewn everywhere. I even painfully knelt on one earlier when I checked for a pulse. It seemed Donna had been wearing an expensive necklace that was ripped from her neck. This reminded me to double check her neck again, I could see some small cuts and scratches near her fingertips.

I decided to stand, careful to avoid stepping on anything. I walked slowly over to the coffee table to take a quick look. Two champagne glasses sat half full, one with lipstick on the rim. I glanced back to Donna, and noticed the color of lipstick she wore matched the color on the rim.

Next to the champagne glasses, I spotted a folded letter sitting on the table top. I didn't want to touch it, so I angled my head till I could see the letterhead.

The correspondence was from a firm named Palmer Properties.

Then the television grabbed my attention. Someone was playing one of those violent war games, and must have been interrupted. The message on the screen clearly showed the game was paused, with the sound off.

And from my new vantage, I saw sitting on the floor next to Donna, opposite from where I knelt to check her, a lone cigar. It was still in the wrapper.

I also noticed, sitting not too far from the television and game system, there was a set of golf clubs standing in the corner, snugly packed in a travel bag.

My curiosity urged me to explore more, but I followed Mae's recommendation and slowly moved back to the entry foyer to leave. Just then a police car pulled up out front, lights blazing. Aunt Mae jumped out and ran up to meet me at the front door. "Why are you still in the house?"

"Aunt Mae, I didn't touch anything, just like you said. I'm just waiting for you."

"Thanks, now go outside on the porch. Wait right there. I'll be right out to join you. I need to ask you a few things. OK?"

"That sounds awful formal, Auntie."

"It is. Just wait out there for a minute." Mae moved

into the old study slowly, and checked for a pulse. I moved out onto the porch, and Mae came out after a few seconds, just like she said she would. "Ginger, darling, are you alright?"

"I'm fine. Better than Donna."

Mae glanced back at the body. "You got that right. So what are you doing here at Donna's?"

"Gypsy, one of Donna's cats, wandered into the Grumpy Chicken. So I brought Gypsy back home. You know we can't have animals running around inside the pub."

"And when did you find the body?"

"Just a minute or two before I called you." I took out my phone, touched the screen a few times, and scanned a list of calls. "Looks like I called you at 12:24."

"Okay. And did you touch anything in the room."

I rubbed my forehead. "No. Well I think I knelt on a pearl when I checked the pulse, but that's it.

"Could you identify the spot where you knelt if you had to?"

"Well, yeah. Just play the knee version of Cinderella. It's the pearl right next to the body, in the impression on the rug that matches my knee ... And, um, I did touch Donna's neck to take her pulse."

"Anything else? Ginger, think hard."

"Well, if you want to count my feet touching the floor?"

"Sure. Walking around in there could have destroyed evidence, do you remember where you walked?"

"Yeah, I went to the body from the front door, looked at couple of things on the coffee table in front of the sofa, and came back to the front door. Really Aunt Mae, are you interrogating me? Those stinking cats in there are contaminating way more than I ever could. And I was careful where I stepped."

"Sweetie, you stomped around in a crime scene. I don't want you getting involved any more than you have to. So I need to know everything you did while you were in there. I wish you had come out of there as soon as we hung up."

"I'm sorry. But it was so shocking and I couldn't help but wonder what happened."

"Let the police handle it, it's not your concern. You have the Grumpy Chicken to take care of, and that is more than a full time job."

"Oh crap, you're more right than you know. I need to get back there. It's Stitch N Bitch Night. We still have a lot to do and I left Dixie and Bones all alone."

"Hang out till Sheriff Morrison gets here, he might have some questions, too. But it won't take long, and I think he's almost here. So you should be able to get back to work in fifteen or twenty minutes." She looked over the top of her nose in a loving way. "It's alright sweetie, I'll wait with you. Dixie and Bones are good employees and will take care of things just fine. And by the way, what's being served tonight for Stitch N Bitch?"

"Buffalo chicken wings, some veg and dip, crackers and cheese, I think some salad, and maybe another app. The usual chips, peanuts and pretzels. And the grill will be open for custom orders."

"Oooo, Buffalo wings. You haven't made those in a while, maybe I should go tonight?"

"Sure, would love to have ya."

"Can I do anything to help ya out?"

"Wear some old clothes. Heavily sauced meats don't go real well with knitting and sewing. It's why we don't make wings that often. But people like them and half the attendees don't craft anyway, they just gossip and drink."

Mae poked me on the shoulder playfully and added, "That's what makes Stitch N Bitch fun, honey!"

Chapter Three

Sheriff Morrison asked the same questions as my Aunt, and after he was done, I hurried back to the Grumpy Chicken. It was now quarter to two and the day was flying by.

When I entered, across the dining area I could see the bald dome of Guardrail towering over every other patron by eight inches. He was sitting at the bar, chatting with Dixie and they seemed awful cozy. I was sure they were talking about that stupid pickled egg jar. I walked over and leaned on the bar next to Guardrail. I had to tilt my head up to look him in the eye. "Hey Guardrail, how's business?"

Guardrail held up his huge right thumb, Caesar style. "Great. Thanks for asking."

I turned to my bartender. "Dixie, I hate to

interrupt, but can I talk to you, in private?"

Her eyes widened, just a bit. "Sure, what's up? You seem a little frazzled."

"We should speak in the back."

After moving to the office in the back of the pub, I made sure no one was lurking outside the door, then closed it. "Sit. ... You're not going to believe this, ... but Donna Holland was killed. I just found her dead!"

Dixie gasped. "Holy sweet molasses crap! I should have sat down like you said. Are you kidding me? The black widow is dead?"

"I touched her neck, took her pulse. She's dead and the cops are there right now."

"Yuck! You better wash and disinfect your hands before touching any food."

"Dixie, focus. I had to tell someone and now I'm not sure I picked the right person."

"Alright! Dang, the rumors are she bumped off her first three husbands to get their money. But now she's dead while getting ready to marry the forth. The irony."

"Donna was only a few years older than me. Took me thirty three years to work on one marriage and get divorced. Jeez. You know, I knew her in high school, she was a junior when I was a freshman."

"OK. Don't wax poetic on me, time for you to stay focused. We got too much drama to deal with right now. So, what are you going to do?"

"Aunt Mae told me to do nothing. So I guess for now – nothing. And you got to promise me to tell no one."

"Okay. I promise.

"Good. Now we need to go on with things as usual, get ready for tonight."

"Me and Bones have it under control."

BAM, BAM! "Hey, you in there? I can't do this all by myself! What's going on in there?" Bones was panicking and as a result I guess he decided to break my office door.

I yelled in response. "What are you doing, you left the register unattended?" I could hear him mutter something and shuffle off back to the dining area. Then I returned to the conversation with Dixie. "I am glad to hear you took care of things, thanks. Bones is right, we should go back to work and try to act normal as possible. Phew, I had to get it off my chest."

"I wish you had picked someone else to tell, to be honest. That is a heck of lot to think about."

"I know, Dixie. Thanks for listening. And by the way, you are doing good with keeping your New Year's resolution not to cuss."

"You have no idea how close I came to breaking it."

I laughed because I knew she wasn't kidding. We left the office and Dixie went back to tending bar. I raced to the kitchen for a quick check on Bones.

"Bones, how many wings you got prepped?"

"Thirty pounds."

"That should be plenty, great."

I moved out into the bar area. "Dixie, you got the citrus cut and …"

Dixie ran towards me, waving her hand in my face. "Ginger, shhh. We got a problem. Look!" She pointed to Beth Givens who was talking non-stop to Guardrail. Beth was the town gossip and had perfect attendance at Stitch N Bitch. She was either late for the early lunch rush, or very early for the upcoming evening's event. "She knows about Donna, saw the cop cars at the Holland house. And somehow, she knows you were there, too! What are we going to say?"

Guardrail saw us, and his voiced boomed over all the other noise. "Ginger, get over here, you pretty red head! I thought we had to talk about replacing the pickled egg jar. But that'll have to wait. I hear you've been busy. Were you out at the Holland place this afternoon?"

There are things I love about small town life.

Actually I love most things about it. But juicy news gets around in a small town faster than a cold in a classroom full of kindergartners. And the way gossip spreads through Potter's Mill is definitely not one of the things I love.

I stayed behind the bar with Dixie and moved over to face Guardrail and Beth. "There are no secrets in Potter's Mill, are there?"

Guardrail shook his head. "Nope. Now spill!"

"There's nothing to tell. I went to return Gypsy, and to let Donna know we can't have her cats getting into the pub."

Beth was smirking the whole time and was waiting to explode, I could tell, but she refrained herself. "Did you really find the body?"

"Yep. No big deal."

That caused an explosion, not from Beth but behind me. Dixie burst, "Monkey farts! No big deal. You found a dead woman Ginger! Sorry. How can you say no big deal?"

Dixie was not usually excitable, but I guess everyone has their limits. Guardrail and I both laughed because it was so unusual for her. Dixie was acting like the one who found the body, guess she was tired from covering both the bar and dining area while I was gone. "Dixie, calm down. It's just something that happened and I was there at the wrong time. I made a phone call and the police are taking care of it. It has nothing to do with us and Deputy Owens told me to stay out of it. I told them what I saw and that's the end of it."

Beth smiled, with pinched lips like she just bit into a real sour lemon. "My goodness, it's been such a long day already. I just helped all the moms sign their kids for up soccer, and now this Donna thing. I could use an adult drink. Dixie, would you be a dear and make me a glass of sweet?"

"Sure, Beth. I just made a new batch of sweet mix." Dixie grabbed a plastic bottle full of mixer to make her drink.

Beth liked margaritas, but for some reason called them sweet. I don't know if it was some southern thing or what, but she was the only person I ever heard call a margarita 'sweet.'

Beth took a sip of her drink, and moaned. "Dixie, my goodness, you sure know how to make sweet. That's good, thank you." In response, Dixie nodded back to indicate you're welcome. Beth continued, "And Ginger, you saw the body, I would love to know more about that. I already have my own list of suspects and would like to know any evidence you may have seen that points to one of them."

"Look Beth, my Aunt Mae was real clear on this, we should all stay out of this and let the police do their job."

"Ah, but you know I know more about the people in this town than anyone. I might be able to help. So you want me to go first, tell you my suspect list?"

I rolled my eyes. "I have a feeling you are going to tell us no matter what I say."

Beth didn't even hear me speak and just kept going. "I need to discuss it out loud, to think it through. You see, there are really only four suspects; Elias Holland, Robert Harlow and his daughter Amber, and last but not least, Silus Palmer."

Guardrail was leaning on the bar with his thick forearm, and pivoted on it to face Beth. "You figured all that out even though the body was only found a couple of hours ago?"

"Of course, dear, it was more than enough time. You see, Robert was planning on marrying Donna. Most of us knew that. But not everyone knew that Donna's stepson Elias would lose his inheritance if she remarried Robert. So, Elias stood to lose a lot if Robert married his step mother. But, if Donna died before getting married again, Elias would get his father's money. So he's definitely a suspect."

I nodded a little. "Okay that makes sense, I guess, but how can Robert and Amber Harlow be suspects?"

"Robert was Donna's lover, her future husband. The lover is always the first suspect. And Amber, whoa, that's a feisty one. Seems she objected to the planned marriage of her father to Donna. On a number of occasions, Amber made her dissatisfaction about it well known, she hated Donna. And it was clear Amber felt her father might end up dead like the first three of Donna's husbands."

Guardrail piped in. "But Amber wouldn't kill someone just for that?"

Beth raised her eyebrows. "She might, her objections were quite strong and some of her comments bordered on threats. She genuinely feared for her father's safety."

I was getting tired of hearing Beth prattle on, so I tried to move her along. "So that's three of your suspects. And the fourth, this Serious Palmer? What about him?"

"It's Silus Palmer, don't you know anything, silly? He's been trying to buy land parcels around Potter's Mill for years. He's trying to build a distribution center for some online retailer, or something. Rumors are swirling that Donna may have been blackmailing him or blocking his efforts to buy land and build. If Donna were blocking Silas' efforts, maybe he finally had enough and retaliated. So he's the fourth suspect."`

I took the empty glass in front of Guardrail and handed it to Dixie. "Well, Beth, I'm glad you figured that all out before the trained law enforcement professionals our town pays to do the job."

Guardrail interrupted, "She makes some good points, Ginger."

"Oh, but now I need your help, dear." Beth repeatedly blinked her eyes at me like a robot rebooting. I think she was trying to say please and couldn't get it out.

I grew tired of waiting for the please from her, so I spoke. "I'm sorry to disappoint, but I really didn't see much. Donna was lying on the floor, I took her pulse, and called the police. End of story."

Beth shook her finger. "Au contraire. For example, I'm guessing you saw what she was wearing?"

"Of course, but I really didn't pay attention. And I spent most of my time standing out on the porch with my Aunt Mae. What I saw was a lot of cats. And not much else."

"Well, was she wearing a wedding dress?"

"No."

"See, you do know some things. Do you remember what else was in the room?"

"Look, Beth, I was told to stay out of this. And I'm not trying to offend you, but I don't want to talk about it anymore."

Beth sighed. "Such a party pooper!"

"Sorry. But I have work to do. It's a busy day for us in the kitchen."

Dog Breath, who was in the custom motorcycle and repair business with Guardrail, came into the pub and took a seat next to his partner. For once in his life, he showed up at a good time, providing cover for me to get away from Beth when he asked, "Ginger, heard you had another jar attacked by the spirit clucker."

Guardrail shook his head. "Dog, you're so far out of the loop. That's real old news, dude. You have to keep up."

"But you just told me about it on the phone ten minutes ago."

Chapter Four

I made some busy work behind the bar and organized some glasses and mugs for Dixie. I was lost in my thoughts. Robert Joseph Harlow is a newcomer to our small town and at the distinguished age of seventy three became Donna Holland's new lover. He has a full head of gray hair and is tall, thin, and always nicely dressed. But what interested me the most, Robert showed up soon after the death of Donna's third husband, Reginald Holland. I hated to admit it, Beth was right. The lover is always suspect number one. I couldn't stop thinking about him and how to find out more about him.

"Hey Ginger, did you really touch the dead body?" Guardrail asked as he picked up his beer.

"Just because you are a big, tough guy doesn't mean you're the only one can who handle being around a dead body. And come to think of it, aren't you the one who climbed up onto that bar stool you're sitting on. You know, that time you thought you saw Gypsy chasing a mouse?" I loved my regulars, but the buzz inside The Grumpy Chicken was brain numbing with the news of Donna's death. I poured a half shot of Jack, and downed it.

Guardrail mumbled to Dog Breath. "What's her problem? She didn't have to bring up the mouse incident."

Dog Breath murmured back to Guardrail. "She has a point. I was here....I've never seen you move so fast."

Guardrail glared back at Dog Breath, and Dog understood, falling silent and he went back to drinking his beer and eating his sandwich. Dixie saw the exchange, and chuckled. "I don't know how you've lived this long making comments like that, Dog. You survived 'Nam, but keep poking your linebacker sized partner's nerves, and you won't see your next birthday."

Dog Breath snorted. "He knows I'm his best friend. He would never ..."

Guardrail poked him sideways with his elbow. "Don't push it. And never bring up the mouse the story again."

"I had to endure Agent Orange and deal with all out assaults in the middle of the Vietnam jungle, but bring up a mouse and, zap, that's it. My long time partner takes me out. That should make for an interesting head stone."

Guardrail chortled, "Who said we would be willing to fork over the money for a headstone?"

"Nice to know I'm loved." Dog took another sip of his beer.

I couldn't help it, with the nervous energy flowing through the pub, my mind couldn't stop thinking about who murdered Donna. "I need some air Dixie. Sorry, but you'll have to hold the fort for a few more minutes."

Guardrail overheard me. "Ah, Ha! See, finding the body did creep you out. Well, there's no shrink in this town to go talk to. But you can talk it out with us."

"You're way off, on two counts. First I am NOT freaked out, but I'm not going to debate my state of mind with you. Second, it's Dixie and I who always dish out the advice in here. If I am going to talk to anyone, it seems that it should be Dixie." I winked at my bartender then I headed out to learn a little more about Robert Harlow.

I walked slowly past a few of the store fronts on Main Street, pondering how I was going to find out more about Donna's new fiance. But small town life gave me a much needed break. Since just about everyone visited our tiny downtown strip during the course of a typical day, I spotted him walking along the sidewalk across the street.

I was in front of the bookstore and ducked inside. Why, I'm not sure but it felt like the right thing to do. I guess it was better if he didn't know I was watching him.

"Well Ginger, so nice to see you out of the pub. You look so pretty with your hair in a pony tail." Edith was alone, looking at a book with motorcycles on the cover. She was usually with her sister Lily and I was a little surprised to see her alone. Edith and Lily were in their seventies, the town's spinsters, and they liked to visit the Grumpy Chicken for their nightly constitution, as they called it. They could be a little wild at times, never married and lived in a stately home just a few blocks from main street. It was a good thing too, neither one of them ever bothered to get a driver's license so they walked everywhere.

I finally answered her. "Thanks. I needed some fresh air." I wasn't lying, that was all she needed to know.

"Well, it seems you were also real interested in Mr. Harlow. You almost walked into the glass door coming in because you couldn't take your eyes off him." Edith smiled at me as she spoke. She may be seventy one, but she didn't miss a thing.

"Well, he's new to town. What do we really know about him?"

Her smile got bigger. "Well, I know he is too old for you. But not for me."

"I'm not sure what to say to that, but ..." I was stammering.

Edith saved me from saying something stupid. "Did you actually find the body?"

"Really? How does word spread so fast in Potter's Mill. I swear, gossip breaks the laws of physics and travels faster than the speed of light here."

"I am not sure about the laws of physics, that is over my head deary, but I'm smart enough to know you're now curious about the lover of a dead woman. Am I right?"

I forced a smile in return. "You're too smart for your own good sometimes, Edith."

"Thank you."

"It wasn't a compliment."

"Oh dear. That tart tongue may be why you've yet to remarry."

"Okay. Truce. Can we change the subject."

"Oooo, look, Robert just came out of Velma's sandwich shop." Edith pointed to him, standing on the sidewalk. We had a good view of him out the bookstore's big glass front door. He was holding a wrapped sandwich in one hand, and patting the pockets of his suit jacket looking for something, with the other.

I shrugged. "It's lunch time. Nothing unusual about that."

"No, I guess not. He's moving. Let's follow him." Edith waved her hand at the exit as she spoke.

"Really?"

"An old fashioned stake out will be fun. Plus, I got some crocheting to work on. I'm making an afghan for my nephew stationed over in Germany. I have everything I need in my tote right here, ready to go." Edith reached down and grabbed the big loop handles of the tote on the floor and held it up for me to see.

"Okay. But you can't tell anyone what we did. Agreed?"

"Agreed."

Robert walked a little, then sat on a bench in front of the bank to eat his sandwich. Edith and I left the bookstore and found a better spot inside the general store a few doors down. It had an old fashioned ice cream parlor, but more important, there were booths that looked out of big windows. We had a perfect view of the bank.

"Freddie, we just need to borrow your booth for a few minutes to chat and crotchet. Is that okay, even if we don't order?"

He nodded. "Sure, Ginger, you are always welcome in here."

"Thanks Freddie!"

We sat with an unobstructed view of the bank. Edith removed the crocheting project from its tote and held it up. "Do you like my afghan?"

"It's very pretty."

Edith began to work the yarn adding rows, or whatever you call them, to the afghan. "Thank you, dear. You should learn to crochet or knit. Lily doesn't do much in the way of crafts either, just like you. Don't know why, she never bothered to get married, which meant she had lots of time to learn."

Edith never married, either, but I wasn't brave enough to point it out. I changed the subject. "Do you think Robert could really be a suspect." I watched as she moved the crotchet hook. It moved in an almost hypnotic rhythm the way she worked with it.

"Oh I don't know. But you know what they say, the murderer always goes to get a sandwich, and then sit in front of the bank, after committing the crime. Oh, and the murderer always dresses nicely, in a suit and tie."

I was intrigued by her matter of fact way of talking about murder, but she was clearly not subjective when it came to Robert. "I think I detected a touch of sarcasm in that last comment."

"Oh, it was much more than a touch, dear."

I laughed at her honestly, then watched Robert brush the crumbs off his suit jacket. He rose, threw the sandwich wrapper into a trash can and checked his pockets again confirming what was inside. After that, he used the bank window as a mirror to check his hair and brushed back a few misplaced strands using his hands, then entered the bank.

"They say he is a successful businessman. Must have some important business with the bank. Don't you think he is handsome?"

"Edith, he's older than my father. He could almost be my grandfather."

"I always say too much. Sorry. But I'm not as bad as Lily. You know she was telling me she saw Robert and Donna in the book store, getting a software, is that what you call it, on how to write your own wills on the computer. They were to marry you know."

"Edith, we all know they were planning on getting married. That's old news."

"Yes, I guess it is. But Lily also said that Robert's daughter, Amber, was there too, arguing with Robert."

"Oh?"

"Oh, yes. Something about it being a mistake. And Amber said something odd. She told Donna that nothing better happen to her father, or that she would make sure Donna paid for her crimes."

"I didn't even hear that one from Beth."

"Lily kept it to herself. Only told me and asked me to keep it secret. Beth is not as well informed as she thinks she is." She frowned at saying Beth's name.

"So why are you telling me now?"

Edith shrugged her shoulders as if annoyed by the question. "Because Donna turned up dead, dear. Might be more important now, don't ya think?"

"I guess."

After about ten or fifteen minutes, or three rows of afghan, Robert came out of the bank holding a receipt. It all looked like he was going about business as usual. Then he turned and started in the direction of the Holland house. "Edith, pack it up. We're going mobile."

We headed out of the general store and down the sidewalk. Edith did not walk fast, so we had to take it slower than I wanted, following Robert as best we could while staying out of sight. After a few minutes, we watched as he saw the lone Potter's Mill police car, as well as a state trooper cruiser and crime van from Savannah, in front of the Holland place. He ran the rest of the way. Sheriff Morrison saw him coming and stopped him. It was kind of far from us, but I observed from a distance as they talked for a moment, and Robert put his hand over his mouth and wailed. I think he may have even cried. Edith and I kept moving closer to the scene and when we were close enough to see better, we looked for a place to stay out of sight.

We took a minute or two and found a hiding spot while the Sheriff consoled Robert. Edith held her hand up in the general direction of the Holland house. "Seems to be pretty normal if you ask me dear. I mean how could a handsome, proper man like that commit a murder? And you see how upset he is?"

I had to admit, Robert didn't seem to be acting like someone who had just murdered another human being. Then his daughter arrived, and I wouldn't use the word normal to describe her behavior. She screamed at Robert, slapped his chest and starting screaming at the police.

"She deserved this. She isn't called the black widow for nothing!" Amber screeched it loud enough for the whole town to hear.

Edith and I were hiding behind a large wooden sign that proclaimed some proposed Main Street development project. We were a couple of hundred feet from the murder scene, but Amber's loud outburst was even heard clearly by Edith. She whispered, "She's pretty upset. That would be suspect number one if you ask me."

The comment made me realize, I know less about her than Robert. Amber walked with difficulty, slightly favoring her left side. No one knew why and we just accepted it. She was a pretty enough woman, mid forties, with blonde hair and blue eyes. Guardrail, Dog Breath, and Digger all made comments about how she was a looker. From what I gathered, she didn't seem to have a career, and skipped from one job to the next. Overall, I thought she was dull and I kept my distance from her. Whenever she came into the Grumpy Chicken, she complained about Donna and the upcoming marriage. She wouldn't let it go and I just figured she was worried about her father. Eventually, I grew tired of hearing it and tuned her out. Now, maybe I should have listened to what she was saying. Could she be the one who murdered Donna? I was a little shocked how fast I went from Robert to Amber as a suspect, but it was hard to argue with what my eyes saw. Amber was acting more like the murder suspect. "Say Edith, we should head back to the Chicken, you know, talk this all through."

"Sure, deary, and would you be willing to grant an old, single lady a drink on the house, too? All this walking and stakeout work is hard on an old body."

I forgot, Edith and Lily shared a gene, the cheapskate one. "Sure, but only one, I have paper thin margins as it is."

"Oh, you J. P. Morgan types, always thinking of your bottom line."

"I'm just trying to stay in business. And the only bottom I worry about is the one I have to squeeze into my jeans."

"Deary, you're so skinny and all the boys like to check out your rump when you're not looking." She nodded just a little, with eyebrows raised, the way people do to let you know they have seen it themselves.

"Again Edith, you've stumped me and I don't know what to say." I may have even blushed a little.

"Say nothing, and let's go, I'm thirsty." And on her own, Edith took a few steps in the direction of the Grumpy Chicken. I guess we were done and heading back.

We leisurely started back for the pub. And if things weren't strange enough already today, as we left, I turned around to take one more look at the scene. The sign we were hiding behind caught my attention. Seems the development announced by the wooded billboard was proposed by Palmer Properties. I saw this particular sign a number of times and never noticed it. But I couldn't miss it now, that was the same name I saw on the letterhead at the murder scene.

Chapter Five

Edith and I made it to the pub in record slow time, and it was now quarter past three. Instead of feeling better, my mind was racing even faster. I wanted to know who murdered Donna. All the signs of a scuffle were there; lamps knocked over and broken, cat tower leaning, feet sliding and scraping on the carpet, and her high-heeled shoes kicked off. Her hands were at her neck in a way that looked like she was fighting to get the cord off her neck and she probably broke her own necklace in the process scattering pearls all over the room. The injured cat I saw could have been stepped on in the chaos. This was not an accident.

But could Amber have done it? I needed someone who could help me get more information about her. Fortunately, I saw Ida and Piper when we entered the pub. Ida had a couple of laptops, and some electronics I didn't recognize. She piped up on seeing me. "Ginger, we got you covered to record the pickled eggs. But where's the new jar."

"Ida, thanks for setting all this up. But I need to talk to you, in private for a few minutes." Piper looked at me like she didn't recognize who she was looking at. I got the message. "You can come too, Piper."

"You look ruffled." Piper was genuinely concerned. I must have looked worse than I thought.

"It's been a long, weird day for sure. Come on, I want to talk with both of you."

Dixie's voice bellowed through the crowded dining room, holding an empty highball glass in the air. "Ginger, Edith says this one is on the house?"

"Yeah, I owe her one." I guess Edith headed straight for the bar while we were talking. She wasn't going to let me have time to rethink my offer.

Ida, Piper, and I headed for the office in back of the pub. After closing the door and getting settled, I told them what Edith and I observed. "I realized, what do we really know about Amber? Who is she? What's her background? Ida, you know how to work the internet, you think you could do a background check on her?"

"Is the Pope catholic?" Ida was back to her cocky

self.

Piper cringed. "What? Are you saying you can do it?"

"Of course I can. How deep you want to go?"

I leaned forward to make sure Ida could see my eyes. "I'm not looking to break any laws, understand. But why couldn't we find out everything we can – legally." I didn't understand hacking, at all, but I sure didn't want Ida doing something that could hurt the Grumpy Chicken.

"Oh, don't worry. Background checks are standard fare, nothing to worry about. Should take me about ten minutes."

"Can you do it right here in the office?"

"Sure. You know that since I installed the wireless network in the pub for you, we can do it here, or just about anywhere in the building."

"Do it. But here in the office so no one sees."

Ida left to get her laptop. I glanced to Piper. "She's good, but I worry about her methods sometimes."

"You should. She told me that she once hacked into the IRS database for a friend."

"See. That's exactly what I'm talking about. How can we make sure she doesn't do something that gets us into trouble?"

"Relax, even I know background checks are SOP these days."

I looked at Piper sideways. "By the way, why are *you* so buddy, buddy with her today?"

"Well, duh, you haven't been available, and Donna's death is big news for Potter's Mill. I'm just trying to get all the inside info I can. It will be the entire front page on my next printing of the Oracle."

Ida returned and sat at my desk. She fired up her laptop, and in just a couple of minutes said, "She is 44, single, never married. Amber Harlow was enrolled in Clemson, studying pre-law. She had a 3.95 GPA. Wow, smart. But she abruptly left school in her last semester, after a bad car accident it seems – and the lawsuits and medical bills bankrupted her."

Piper added, "Hmm, car accident. That could explain the limp. And sounds like she had a serious issue in that last semester of college. Like gambling or drugs?"

The office door flew open. It was Dixie. "I hate to break up the sisterhood of the traveling thumb drive, but are you going to do any work today, Ginger? Bones and I are barely keeping up with the crowd out there that is growing with all the talk about Donna."

"Dixie, we had to check something out. Is Bones watching the register?"

Dixie cocked her head. "Yep. Now what is so important to let so many customers wait."

Ida blurted out, "Amber may have killed Donna."

"Flash Gordon's nipples!"

The three of us stared at Dixie. I held my hands in the air. "Where do you get your cuss words? Do you stay up at night and write them down?"

"No! I just say what comes to mind."

"And Flash Gordon and nipples was the first thing to enter your brain?"

Dixie's face went blank. "Yeah, not that bad eighties movie, the old TV series with the bad special effects. And you know, the news about Amber was kind of a news flash, so … "

I couldn't keep from chuckling as I cut her off, "Oh my goodness. You need help."

Ida had enough time to pull up a YouTube clip from the movie, and we heard music start followed by 'Flash! Ahhhhh.' All of us burst into a full belly laugh, except Dixie, and we probably let it go on longer than we should. "Oh come on, it's funny, sweetie."

Dixie flinched, like she was going to stomp her foot, but she caught herself. "Bull sh…. shampoo!

It's funny only if you had all day off from work. Are you going to help us or play Inspector Clueso all day? Don't forget, we got Stitch N Bitch tonight."

I wiped the tears from my eyes. I needed a good laugh. But I felt bad for Dixie. "You know what, you're right. You're right. We're being silly."

Ida's tone changed. "Oh my! This is interesting. I got some of Amber's Facebook posts here. Seems she told some of her friends back home that she is very worried about her father's safety. Accused Donna of being a murderer. And if anything happened to Robert, Amber said she would make Donna pay for it."

Piper noted, "It sounds like she was bad mouthing Donna everywhere." Piper was thinking out loud and starting to see Amber as a suspect, I could see it in her eyes.

I wasn't laughing any more. "And it's what she blurted out at the murder scene. She said Donna would pay for being a black widow. Seems she was fixated on Donna and the death of her previous three husbands. But nothing happened to her father, so why would she kill Donna?"

"Simple. Preemptive strike." Piper was in journalist mode now. "Well, that, and maybe she was getting money from her father, and that's why she stays close to him. Maybe he's the only reason she can make ends meet at all. If she lost him, she might go bankrupt again. Maybe? Took Donna out to protect her cash cow."

Ida chimed in. "Yeah. Her credit does stink. Looks like she has had serious money problems since the car accident. Maybe she is still an addict or something, and just managing it from day to day."

"Have you actually looked at the woman? She never drinks more than a glass or two of wine, and never hard liquor ... her eyes are clear and bright ... plus she's still pretty smart if you actually talk to her. And if you asked her the difference between a football and a race horse, I honestly don't think she could tell you. She isn't an addict or a gambler." I hated shooting them down, but I knew they were wrong. We had to look for something else.

Ida typed some more. "I can dive a little deeper, but it will take me a few minutes." She seemed to shrink into her laptop screen.

Piper was fiddling with some coaster samples sent to me for evaluation. "These are nice. Why don't you use these instead of those crappy cardboard ones?"

"Because they cost ten times as much and I don't have that kind of money."

"You shouldn't be giving away drinks to old ladies then."

"Edith helped me out today. It was the least I could do to thank her."

"And did she help you?"

"She shared some things Lily overheard."

"You trying to replace Beth as the town gossip?"

"Heck, no. I'm just curious who could have done this. You know, after being the one to find Donna dead."

"I guess that's understandable. But if the New York Times wants your story after you figure it out, you tell them you promised the exclusive to The Potter's Mill Oracle."

"You know we frown on anything from the Big Apple here. I would give my story to the Washington Post. They scooped Watergate, so they should handle this with no problem." I smiled, but she eyed me back like the fox in her hen house. I added, "Of course! I'm just teasing ya, Piper!"

"Not – funny – at – all." Piper could make a long face on cue like no one else.

"Bingo!" Ida sat up and plunked her hands on either side of the laptop. "Look at this. She is being audited and owes back taxes. That would keep Sleeping Beauty awake at night."

"Ida, please tell me you did nothing illegal to find out about the taxes."

"No, I got into her email and saw an accountant asked her to confirm some information for the audit.

Well hacking someone's email might be technically illegal, but no one cares about getting into email. Usually."

"Okay, you found enough for today. Please stop. I don't want the internet police tracing illegal activity back to my pub."

"Oh, don't be silly, I bounced the encrypted connection through a special VPN that bounces the tunnel around. As long as the top level guys at NSA don't get involved, we're fine."

"I'm not sure what all that is. But you need to stop, now, please."

"Alright." She sighed as if she was eight years old and I took her favorite toy away.

Piper thought out loud again. "This is all interesting, but what do we do with the information? And are we the only ones who know?"

"Well, Aunt Mae told me not to get involved. But we just learned something she may want to know. I guess I should go tell her to make sure the police have the information." I was actually thinking out loud, too, looking for reassurance.

"If you tell her, she might ask how you found out." Ida was worried I would out her not so elaborate hacking operation.

"Don't worry. I will just tell Auntie that it's things I heard in the pub."

"Well if you heard it in the Grumpy Chicken, aren't the odds the police probably heard it too?" Piper seemed to be with Ida on this one.

"No, we should help if there is any chance that the information will be useful. It's our civic duty."

Ida scowled. "I'm not sure it is our civic duty. And I don't like bringing information from a hack to the police."

"They will never know it was you, I promise." I knew Mae would understand and not ask too many questions about who said what over drinks at the Grumpy Chicken. The decision was made, I was going to visit the police station.

Chapter Six

The police station sat at the very end of what we called the downtown strip. It was section of Main Street where most of the stores and businesses were located, including the Grumpy Chicken. I walked from the pub to the old building that housed our small police force in a little over ten minutes.

Eunice Houston, the young daughter of Bessie and Carl who owned Sew Fabric, worked behind the reception desk. "Hello Ginger. What brings you here on this busy day."

"I need to speak to my aunt."

"Mae is speaking to someone in the conference room, but you can wait at her desk. You know where it is."

"Thanks Eunice." I made it to Mae's work station and took a seat on the side of her desk, then studied the pile of papers in the middle of the desktop. We don't have many murders in Potter's Mill. Come to think of it this was the first I knew of, and it seems the crime of murder creates a lot of paperwork.

"Well sweetie, what are you doing here?" Mae approached from behind as she spoke.

I spun to face her. "I thought you were talking to someone."

"I was just sitting in with the Sheriff during an interview. But I saw you come in. What'ya need, honey?" She made her way to the seat at the desk and sat.

"Actually, I have something for you."

"Oh really?"

"I overheard a number of comments in The Chicken, and I thought I should tell you about them. They might relate to the murder."

"First, no one has officially said it was murder. And second, I told you not to get involved."

"Sure, Aunt Mae, but everyone is talking about it. And I heard some things about Amber Harlow that you should know."

"Alright."

"Seems she has been real worried about her father getting married to Donna. That he may end up dead like her first three husbands."

"Honey, we all know that. Amber told anyone who would listen."

"Yeah, but in addition she has *real* serious money problems it seems."

"Oh?"

"Also, she was being audited by the IRS. And I saw her at the Holland house not long after I found the body. She was irrational, emotional, and seemed kind of unhinged."

"Just what are you saying?"

"Um, Potter's Mill doesn't have a murder, well, never. Amber shows up with her father, with real bad money problems, worried about her father being dead husband number four claimed by the black widow. Seems like she might have had a reason to want Donna dead. And she is an emotional wreck, almost irrational. She might be a suspect. I just wanted to let you know."

"Ginger, you are a real sweet girl and I don't want you getting yourself involved in this. It's dangerous and you could get hurt. So just say no to anyone who wants to pull you into this investigation. Leave it to the police. The state police are sending some people to help us, too. We got this well covered."

"Auntie, I'm not getting involved. Just passing on what I heard."

"Sweetie, I'm a town deputy. I can put two and two together. You be careful what you do with that Ida who hangs around the pub. The FBI called us once, asked about her. Wanted to know if she ever got into trouble here. Seems they didn't have enough to charge her, but they knew she might have hacked into an IRS computer."

"Well that's troubling."

"Sure is. And I don't want you getting hurt or finding trouble. Even worse, you might interfere with our efforts. You don't want to hurt our investigation do you?"

"Of course not."

"Good. Now I know you found the body, but put this all out of your mind and don't worry about it. We got it handled." Mae patted the big pile of papers on her desk to emphasize her point. "And I don't think Amber is a murderer."

"How can you say that."

"First, we know everything you told me. It's normal for people to have a bad stretch in their life. Seems she had an extraordinary streak of bad luck in her last year of college, including a car wreck, and has struggled ever since. She has worked hard to stay afloat and is nice girl."

"You found all that already?"

"We're the police, it wasn't hard, honey. And as for her bad mouthing Donna, wouldn't you?"

"What do ya mean?"

"Donna was thirty six. Robert was seventy three. That means Robert was thirty seven years her senior. Kind of unusual, don't you think?"

"I think it's gross, to be honest. Donna was only three years older than me."

"Right! And Amber probably did too. Plus Donna has three previous husbands now taking dirt naps. Seems to me I would worry about that, too, if my father was going to marry her."

"I guess."

Mae continued, "It makes perfect sense. And in addition, she was hurt, bad, in her car accident. I don't think she is strong enough to choke herself, let alone another person."

"I didn't think of that."

"See, leave it to us, the professionals. Please, honey. You need to stay out of this."

"Okay. I was just trying to do my civic duty and bring information forward that I thought would help."

"That's sweet, sugar. But you need to run your pub

and take what you hear in there with a grain of salt. The gossip in that place is awful."

"Tell me about it. And I've left Bones and Dixie alone almost all day. I feel bad and should head back to give them a hand."

"There ya go, good girl. I might see you tonight, but who knows. We're pretty busy today."

"I understand. Hope to see ya there though." I rose and kissed her on the cheek. "You're always so patient and kind with me. Thanks Auntie."

"You're welcome sweetie."

I left the station feeling like an idiot, a little more humble than when I had entered. But the days seemingly random events were not ready to leave me alone. Amber was sitting on a bench in front of the station and my new found humility was gone in a blink. I couldn't let the opportunity pass and I sat down next to her.

"Hello, how are you doing?" I was trying my best not to assume she was the killer and just chat with her.

"How do ya think? My father's fiance was just murdered. I hate her. But I don't need this kind of aggravation."

"I know. This must be hard for you."

Amber snapped, "How could you know?"

"I guess I couldn't, you're right. I never experienced anything even close. I'm sorry."

Amber sniffled. "I'm sorry too, I shouldn't have been curt with you. It's been too much for me to take today, my nerves are shot."

"I can only imagine." I tried to pick my words more carefully to prevent her from being riled again.

"You want to ask me, don't you? Everyone else does."

"What?"

"You want to know if I killed her."

I studied her face for a moment, then asked, "Well, did you?"

"Why do you care about that crazy cat lady enough to wonder who killed her?"

"Well, for starters it means we have a murderer walking among us in Potter's Mill."

"Why weren't you concerned about Donna then. She killed three husbands."

"That was never proven and no charges were ever filed after thorough investigations."

Amber snorted. "Thorough! I don't think so. She was as guilty as could be. You went to high school with her didn't you?

"Yeah."

"Doesn't it bother you that your little town produced a serial killer? No! But you ask me if I killed her. They told me small town southerners stick together."

"It's that this just happened. Everyone is wondering who killed Donna and wants to find the murderer."

"Well, it wasn't me or my father. We are decent people who were just trying to move on with our lives and make a better place in the world."

"I'm sorry. I didn't want to upset you."

"Really? You asked me if I committed a murder, but didn't think that would upset me?"

"Sorry, I should have thought that through a little more before asking. I tend to be pretty direct. I know I need to work on that." I could feel the pain and confusion she was dealing with. "Is there anything I can do for you?"

"Just leave us alone. I can't deal with all the staring eyes and questions."

"Then why are you sitting on a bench outside the police station?"

"The Sheriff brought us in for questioning, I just got out and took a seat to wait for may father. He's still talking to the Sheriff."

"I see, then I will respect your wishes and leave you alone. And seriously, if you need anything, please let me know and I will do whatever possible to help."

"That's nice of you, thanks."

"By the way, we're making wings tonight. Do you like Buffalo chicken wings? It will be supper time in an hour or two, can I bring some over to your place so you don't have to cook or worry about dinner tonight?" I was overcompensating, but guilt for being so direct with her got the best of me.

"We're good, thanks. I was at Daryl Reid's office all morning, finalizing some business with him for my father. He invited me and father over for dinner. I'm pretty sure we will cancel now, but ..."

"Wait! You were at his real estate office all morning? Can Daryl confirm that?"

"Sure. He already did to the police."

Now I understood why the police released her and why Mae was so confident Amber didn't commit the murder. She had a strong alibi.

Chapter Seven

Customers trickled in all afternoon for a bite to eat and something to drink. But today the food and drinks were an afterthought. Locals knew The Grumpy Chicken was the prime spot to learn of Potter's Mill news and it didn't get any bigger than the murder of Donna Holland. I saw we were close to capacity in the dining room.

It was just after five o'clock when I returned and all of the expected regulars were here, plus a few surprise guests. One I noticed in particular, Donna's stepson, Elias Holland, sat at the bar chewing on Dixie's ear.

"You've no idea. It's complicated, but there is only one person who wanted her dead – Amber Harlow." Elias had been drinking as evidenced by a couple of slurred words.

Dixie had her fake sympathetic bartender voice going. "Sweetie, I just serve the drinks. Let's leave the detective work to the police."

"And that crazy woman has no idea that she probably killed me too." Elias slapped the bar top and frowned. "How can life suck so bad!"

"Easy, honey. It always looks bleakest before the dawn." Dixie used that line a little too often.

"No! Like I said, you don't understand."

"What don't I understand?"

"My father was a great man. Well, I hated him like most sons do ... in some ways ... but he was a good man. I was supposed to get his money. But Donna made him change it so she got the money if he died. I only got the money if both of them kicked the bucket."

"See, there ya go. You're in line for a big pay day. Getting a big check isn't going to kill ya."

"That's what is supposed to happen. But with Donna's engagement to Robert, it's way more complicated than you know. I don't know what I'm going to do."

"Ah, you're just upset and that's understandable. You've had a pretty traumatic day. But don't worry, it'll all work out."

"We'll see. Can I have another one?" Elias waggled his empty glass.

"You sure? You've had a few and your tab is getting pretty big?"

"Give me another." Elias plunked the empty glass on the bar like a judge hammering a gavel, just to make it clear he was sure.

Then I saw Bessie Houston enter with empty hands and it looked odd. She always carried some project to work on while she talked. Even more strange, Stitch N Bitch didn't start until seven o'clock – Bessie was not known to be early.

"Ginger, dear, can we talk." Bessie was fidgeting with her hands while she spoke.

"Sure."

"With all that's happened, should we cancel tonight?"

I was paying more attention to the customers being served, but now Bessie had my full attention. "Why, most of the time we chat and exchange gossip anyway. This would be a perfect night for Stitch N Bitch."

"Oooo. Sorry, but you know I don't like that name." She even grimaced at hearing it. "I know you do a lot of work to get ready for us, but Carl and I were talking. We don't want to seem disrespectful."

I held both hands up. "Bessie, look around, the place is packed. People are looking to get out and talk to each other. It'll be fine."

"Well, that's just it. No one wants to talk about crafting. They want to talk about ... who did it."

"That's probably true."

"So why don't we just cancel the function and Carl

and I won't seem like we are trying to profit from Donna's death."

"I see now." I was so focused on my hectic day, I stopped being a considerate human being. She had a good point.

Bessie smiled. "And besides, we have something that doesn't happen very much around here. There's a mystery to figure out."

My voice raised a little when I said, "A mystery? It's an actual murder, not an episode of Murder She Wrote."

"Well, you know how the boys are around here. A pool will start before too long, if it hasn't already, and they'll make silly bets on who did it. And there will be four or five theories that are popular, but a bunch of wild ones too. That is where everyone will be focused – who did it and why. And they will all think they have solved the mystery and argue over who is right. It is better for us to cancel, just step aside, and let things play out."

"I don't know."

"We'll pay for the food you've prepared, that's not what you're worried about, is it?

"No, Bes. I'm not worried about that. I just wanted to keep things, well, normal."

Bessie laughed. "Sweetie, that's out of your control today. Things are about as abnormal in Potter's Mill as can be today."

"I guess you're right. Okay, we'll cancel."

"Great. Carl and I will still be coming tonight. What are you making?"

"Buffalo wings."

"Yummy! Love your wings. Oh, and one more thing sweetie, Carl and I have a large whiteboard we used before we installed the new flat screen to show our specials. You can have the old whiteboard if you want, it might be of use to show your specials."

"That is very kind of you, thanks. But ..."

Bones was bussing a nearby table and overheard us talking. "Hey boss, maybe you can put that whiteboard up on that big blank wall outside the office, ya know next to the walk in cooler."

"And what am I going to use it for there?"

"Well, things we need to get, like a shopping list. And planned menus. And to do lists. So, stuff like that. Or maybe we can even list the odds that Dog is coming up with for the murder suspects." Bones paid attention more than I thought.

"Bones, you know as an established business we can't even seem to have a part in gambling. And why would I do anything like that when it's one of our own that's been murdered? It's disrespectful."

"Ginger O'Mallory!" Guardrail always used my last name when he thought he had a good idea or wanted my attention. He must have been eavesdropping. "Bessie has made a generous offer. And Bones is right, we can use it to work on solving the whodunit."

"For such a big guy, sometimes I wonder about the size of your brain. I can't do anything that will look like we are gambling or taking advantage of the situation."

Guardrail pointed. "Look at Dog Breath and Digger over there. They're arguing about whether Amber did it. Digger says Amber did it, but has no idea why other than she was outspoken. And Dog says there's only a zero to one percent chance she did it because he's certain it's a professional hit man. My fool of a partner has seen too many movies and thinks only assassins commit murders. Well, that and maybe too much time with the degreasing solvent at the shop."

I retorted, "Dog also thought the pub was haunted by General Sherman after he watched the PBS special on the civil war. What's your point?"

"People want to talk about this, exchange ideas. They're not being disrespectful. It's only natural to want to know who did it, and why. You would be doing a service and just giving the people what they want."

"No, that's not something I can do. How would you like it if your name was on a board for all to see as a potential murderer? We know these people."

"What? Are you saying I'm a suspect, too?

I chuckled. "See, not a good feeling is it? But come to think of it, maybe we should take a closer look at where you were this morning. You do seem to be acting a little odd." I eyed him, then smacked my forehead. "But what was I thinking, that's not unusual for you."

"You think you're funny?" Guardrail tried to sulk at me, but his attempt failed.

I tired to hide my laughter, "Alright. Sorry, didn't mean to offend, just messing with ya." I turned back to Bessie. "But however, Bessie, I'll take the board. I can use it in the pub to post things to do, specials, stuff like that." I couldn't let the offer go. I knew we could use the board, just like Sew Fabric used it, and there was no way I could afford to buy one on my own.

Bessie replied. "Okay. Glad to see it used. It's just collecting dust in our backroom now."

Guardrail volunteered, "Me and Dog will go get it, put it up for ya."

"I said it wasn't for solving the crime, got it." I knew Guardrail had an idea and the whiteboard was part of it. I may have made a mistake by accepting Bessie's hand-me-down.

"Got it." Guardrail spun and yelled over the crowd

noise. "Dog, drink up. We got a quick job to do!"

Dog looked up, foam still on his lip. "I just ordered another one."

"It'll be there when we get back. Dixie, put that beer for Dog on hold till we get back." Guardrail waved at her in thanks, then he and Dog headed out.

I continued with Bessie, "Do you have an opinion on who may have done it?" I was curious if she was also caught up in the mania. Carl and Bessie were long time residents, and usually level headed, making them good test subjects to see how deeply the town was obsessed with the murder.

"Oh yes. I think it may have been suicide. No one in this town could have done it. Me and Carl know everybody, and everyone here is just too nice to have done it." Bessie smiled after presenting her theory.

I had no idea that the town wasn't only obsessed with the murder, it was losing its mind. "Well, that is … is … different Bessie." I couldn't think of anything else to say.

Without warning, there was a strange buzzing sound and everything went dark. A deafening high pitched "Gharrrrrrrk!" filled the pub. And after only a few seconds, the lights came back on. The dining room noise went from loud crowd noise to silence in a heartbeat. I realized Bessie was hanging on to my arm.

After a long pause, a lone quivering voice broke the silence, "Ghostly poultry!" Lily's eyes were wide and her jaw hung.

"That's the first time the chicken has squawked in the dining room. And during the day!" Digger was looking at the ceiling for some reason as he spoke.

"Bones, check the fuse box." I waved at him to go and look. "It's alright, everyone, this is a real old building. It's probably just an overloading of the fuses from the new deep fryer."

"Ginger, we all heard it. That was the sound of a chicken spirit. And it sounded like it's head was being lopped off." Edith's face was white.

"No, it sounded like an electrical fuse burning out. I'm sure Bones will find it."

Bones yelled from the rear of the pub. I barely heard him. "Boss, you should see this!"

"Excuse me." I went into the kitchen and moved to the rear of the building. Bones met me outside the old walk-in cooler.

"Take a look at the wings." Bones' voice was more of a whisper now and he pointed at the cooler door.

"Okay." I entered the cooler and bent over the bucket filled with thirty pounds of brined chicken wings. They were a vibrant lime green and a few wings floated on surface in an unnatural way.

Bones walked in behind me. "See that Boss? That's the weirdest green I've ever seen. I just checked these last hour and they were fine. And there is no smell."

"What is … is that an 'R' on top formed by some bubbles? That can't just be a coincidence." I stuck the tip of my index finger into the green brine then raised it to my nose and sniffed the liquid. It smelled like fresh chicken.

"I don't know what it is. And there's no way I'm touching it. It's cursed now. You shouldn't touch it either, Boss."

"Thanks for sharing that now that I stuck my finger in it." I glared at Bones. "Don't tell anyone about this. Say a fuse blew in the panel. Actually, did any fuses blow?"

"Nope. All just fine."

"Well if anyone asks, a fuse blew and made the lights go out. The noise was the fuse failing. Got it?"

"Sure. If you say so."

We heard a clamor outside of the cooler, and exited to find Guardrail and Dog already back with the large whiteboard, plus a box full of markers and erasers. They brought the load through the back door and set it down.

"Where do you want it installed?" Guardrail was apparently ready to use the new toy.

"Hang it right here, for now." I pointed to a large blank space on a wall just outside the office.

"Can do. We know where your tools are and it will take ten or fifteen minutes." Guardrail was talking fast. He always talked quickly when he worked.

"Doesn't have to be put up in record time. Just do it right. I don't want it falling off the wall."

"Come on! It's me and Dog, you couldn't have two better installers."

"That's exactly what I'm worried about. How many beers has Dog had? And you too. Come to think of it, there was only one sign that fell over when the last tropical storm blew through here. Wasn't that the sign for your shop?"

"Yeah, but 'we' didn't install it." Guardrail glared sideways to Dog Breath.

Dog shot back, "What? I did it myself because you weren't around."

Chapter Eight

Guardrail and Dog finished installing the whiteboard in fifteen minutes. And true to their word, it was done right. The wall would fall over before the whiteboard would fall off.

"So can I break her in?" Guardrail looked like a child substituting a broad smile for the word please.

I held out my hand towards the newest addition to the pub. "Go ahead, you big kid. You earned it. But keep it clean."

"I always do, well most of the time." Guardrail took a marker from the box and wrote something real fast.

Dog laughed at it and shook his head. "You got it all wrong, man." Then he picked up a marker, and added something of his own.

I glanced at what they were so intently marking on the board. "You sons of a beer can! I said no gambling!"

Dog jerked back. "It isn't gambling. We're just listing the odds on who's the killer."

I took an eraser from the box and tried to erase the list of names, along with odds. But they stubbornly refused to come off. "Why won't this erase?"

Bones said, "Old board and markers, I guess. You'll have to use some water and a rag." He followed up on his own suggestion by getting a wet dish cloth from the sink and cleaning the board. "See, it just needs some TLC."

I pointed to a spot on the board. "I can still see what they wrote."

Guardrail chimed in, "That's whiteboards for ya. Sometimes the faint image of what you wrote just stays."

"So a custom motorcycle slash repair guy is also a whiteboard expert?"

"You don't have to be so crabby. Don't get worked up about it, you can hardly see it. Plus it's in the back where only you can see it."

"Come to think of it, you're right. Thanks for hanging the board. Now you and Dog need to go back to the bar. This is an employees only area."

"Ah, don't be mad at us – and we're here so much we're almost employees. Who's the likely killer is what everyone is talking about anyways." Dog was too fixated on this odds making thing.

"Git!" I waved toward the swinging door out to the dining room.

Guardrail and Dog Breath left the kitchen and went back to their drinks and gossip. Bones and I stared at each other for a few seconds.

"Well, Boss, what are we going to do with all those chicken wings?"

"Can't use 'em. We'll just have to throw them out."

Bones raised his eyebrows and made a long face. "Wow! That's a lot of meat to waste."

"What else can we do? Just do it. And if anyone asks why we decided to take the wings off the menu tonight, just tell them the bin got knocked over and we had to trash them."

"Can do, boss. But I'm not touching the wings or liquid."

"Just dump it in the dumpster. Alright?"

"Kay." Bones grabbed the bucket and took it out back to dispose of the wings.

I went into the office to think and undid the rubber band holding my pony tail. I brushed my hair a few times, then pulled it into a pony tail again and tied a fresh white ribbon around it. Then I went into the kitchen and checked the grill to make sure there were no forgotten orders or anything burning. After filling a couple of orders, I walked back to the dining room to find the crowd noise was back, louder than before. And the number of people seemed larger. But I noticed an empty spot where Elias Holland sat earlier. "Dixie, did Elias square up before he left."

"No! And he stiffed me on the tip."

"That's not like him. But we'll just have to make sure he makes it up to ya some how."

Dixie waved me over closer to her, behind the bar. Once I got there, she whispered to me. "Ginger, what the hell was that lights business, and that noise?"

"Don't know, but let's not get crazy. Nothing is broken and no one got hurt, so don't worry about it. It might scare some of the customers if we fixate on it. And by the way, does 'hell' count as a cuss word?"

Dixie glared at me. "Really! That's what you are going to focus on, my cussing and the dollar jar? And what is don't worry about it? Are you serious? That's just horse ..."

"Ginger!" Edith's voice somehow made it over the noise and she was waving to make herself visible. So I took her invitation to leave Dixie to her drink making.

"What can I do for you two young ladies?" I picked up some empty glasses off the table.

"We were just talking, about what you and Edith saw today." Lily looked deep in thought.

I may have made a mistake coming over to talk with them. "Well, it wasn't much."

Lily continued "I don't like that Amber girl. Always thought she was off."

"How so? Think about it, Amber has a lot on her dinner plate. Her father was thirty seven years older than Donna. And even Amber is twelve years older than her. It was an odd engagement if you ask me. And Amber was worried that her father would become Donna's dead husband number four."

Edith added,"But she seemed to be really upset and incoherent at the murder scene. Yelling at the police and all."

"Yep. She was upset. But I don't think she murdered Donna." I wasn't going to tell them about the alibi the police were privy to.

Lily huffed. "Well who did it then?"

"I don't know."

Edith pondered, "What about Elias. We saw him in here earlier, drinking too much. And he was saying he was in danger of being killed himself. Amber and Elias didn't get along at all and now he is afraid of her? Seems to me like she is the prime suspect."

"No. He just said he could turn up dead, too, and it would be Amber's fault. That's different from being afraid of her. Honestly, I don't think it's her, but who knows. And what do we know about Elias? He's real upset too."

Lily paused to consider the thought. "I guess. And

we are talking about a lot of money he stands to inherit."

"See! ... Wait a minute. That's a good point. Even Elias said he didn't know if things would go as he expected. What did that really mean? And what do we know about him?"

Edith replied. "He's lived here a while, now. And since the death of his father, we never see him much. He plays those stupid video games all day."

"Exactly, we hardly ever see him except when he comes to the pub for a few drinks. What's he been up to?" I swiveled my head, and found the two I people I needed. "Excuse me, ladies, I need to talk with Piper and Ida."

In unison, the sisters kvetched. "We're boring you?"

"No, that's not it, but I need to ask them something real quick. Excuse me."

I moved through the crowd over to Piper and Ida then took a seat at their table. "What mischief are you two making?"

"What do you think?" Ida never looked up from her screen.

Piper eyed my hair and said, "I like the ribbon. The white goes good with your red hair."

I turned to Ida, "Well, anything new?"

Ida finally looked up and took a sip of her drink. "Nope, been doing a little more digging, but looks like we found most of Amber's life story. Strange a pretty girl like her never got married."

Piper rubbed her ear like it was blocked. "Ginger, what was with the lights, and that noise?"

"Just a fuse blowing out." I wasn't going to tell them the truth out in the dining room where someone else might hear.

"It was real strange." Piper scrunched up her face. "I never heard anything like that and I have no idea what it was."

"Don't worry about it. It was a fuse blowing. Focus, I want to talk about Elias."

"What?" Ida had drifted back to the laptop screen, but looked up at hearing his name.

"He stands to inherit money. And they always say to follow the money. But I heard him say it's complicated, and he wasn't sure what would happen."

"So." Ida waved off my comment.

I paused for a moment, then blurted it out. "So, what if he lost his inheritance when Donna remarried. Then he would have a motive to kill her *before* she married Robert."

Piper gasped. "Whoa! That's unbelievable. But

how did we not think of this till now?"

I nodded. "I know. But maybe we should do a background check on him too?"

Ida began typing. "I can do that. Let me see."

"No! Not here. In the office, like before with Amber. I don't want anyone to see what we're doing."

"OK. Worry wart!" Ida had a drink and burger and apparently did not want to leave them. She picked both up and balanced it all along with her laptop.

"Thanks. I'll meet you there in a second." I cleaned a few tables and grabbed some plates from the order window to deliver to customers. It was the least I could do. I was gone most of the day and Dixie and Bones were being asked to do a lot. Finally, things seemed to be caught up and I went back to the office. On entering, Piper was sitting on the corner of my old desk watching Ida, who was seated behind the desk working her laptop.

"You little hypocrite." Piper was smiling at me.

I shot back, "What? Don't call me a hypocrite, unless you are swearing me in to be a doctor!"

"Miss smarty pants. You couldn't resist. We saw your list on the new whiteboard."

"I didn't write that. Guardrail and Dog did."

Piper smiled, "Sure they did."

"They did! So what did you find?"

Ida kept typing but interrupted, "This is going to be tougher than it was for Amber. Elias is obviously more computer savvy than her and I need to dig a little."

"Nothing illegal. Nothing!"

"Do you want to know or not?"

"I want to know what we can find out about Elias legally. And if you do anything illegal, I don't want to know about it but I will ban you from the pub."

Ida snorted. "Oh come on, you would never ban me."

"Yes I would. Don't do anything illegal while on my network."

Ida chuckled at my insistence. "OK, but you're taking all the fun out this."

Piper went into journalist mode. "Why have you moved on to Elias anyway?"

"His comments at the bar were interesting, if not strange. But Edith also told me that she saw Robert and Donna looking at software to write wills. If Donna did change her will, his comments along with the possible loss of big piles of money make him a pretty good suspect."

Ida scratched her head. "If they wrote a will, they would have to appoint an executor. I might be able to find that out."

Piper added, "And maybe they sought out legal help at some point?"

Ida nodded in agreement. "We should be able to find something, yeah." She plucked a few more keys, then, "You gotta love email. I searched Robert's inbox for 'executor' and bingo! An executor was named, they asked Robert's lawyer in Atlanta to handle it."

I was unimpressed. "So what? Does that mean anything?"

Ida typed some more. "I don't know, yet. Hang on."

Piper asked, "Ginger, what did you see in the room? How was she killed?"

"With a headset cord."

"Where did the headset come from?"

I paused and finally said, "Good question. Maybe from the gaming system."

"From a game system?"

"Could be. I saw a game remote on a bean bag chair. And a video game was paused on the TV."

Piper exhaled, then said, "And Elias was known to

be an avid gamer."

I slowly nodded yes. "Yeah, he talked about it at the bar often."

Piper asked, "What game was it?"

"I don't know. Why"

Ida jumped in. "Those games have live recording and all kinds of chat rooms. I might be able to find some dirt on Elias through the game."

Piper added, "Ask Dog. Elias talked to Dog a lot about a war game he played."

"And it was a war game I saw paused. Keep working, I need to go chat with Dog for a minute."

I left the office and made my way to the bar. It was crowded, so it was easier for me to go behind the bar and approach Dog Breath seated at his usual bar stool, head hanging over his half filled beer mug.

Dixie stopped me. "Well, look who has reappeared from play time in her office. I'm still worried ya know, we need to talk!"

"I know, but not now, I need to do something." I was now directly across from Dog. "Dog, I need to know what video game Elias talked to you about, the one he played all the time."

Dog looked up from his beer. "Why do you want to know that?"

"I just do. Tell me."

"Elias would often ask me questions about what real war was like, in 'Nam. You know. He was trying to beat that darn game."

"Dog, I know you fought in Vietnam, but I asked a simple question. I need to know what game it was."

Dog seemed to go into a trance, "I told him all about the real deal. How you really survive in the jungle."

I was fidgeting. "Dog, please focus, what game did Elias play all the time."

Guardrail came to my rescue. "Dog, flashback time is over. The pretty lady asked you a question. Can you answer it?"

"Sure. Elias played Call of Duty."

I touched his hand. "Thanks Dog." Then I headed back to the office with the new information.

I entered and re-closed the door. I blurted out, "Call of Duty. He played Call of Duty."

Ida responded, "Got it. We should have guessed, that's pretty popular. Let me see what I can find." Ida tapped on the keyboard for about five minutes while we waited in silence.

Piper finally asked, "Ida, anything?"

Ida glared at Piper. "Patience, a master is

working." Ida went back to her keyboard, then added. "Well, well, well! Look at this. Elias did play online live with a group and they chatted often. In one those chats, he said, and I quote, he hated Donna and would kill her before she remarried anyone else."

I actually gasped. "Elias is looking more like a strong suspect."

Piper added, "And get this, we found a little more when you were gone."

Ida continued, "Yeah, seems Robert was a little more careless than Elias with his computer habits and attached a draft of the will to an email. Robert got Donna's money if she died, and vice versa. That seems pretty standard with spouses. But look at this, the money was to be split between Elias and Amber if both Robert and Donna died."

Piper sarcastically added, "So get this, Elias doubled his money if Donna died before she remarried. By the way Ida, how much money are we talking?"

Ida tilted her head. "Let me see if I can find something."

I asked, "So Amber gets no money if Donna dies before she remarried?"

Ida said, "Well, yeah, I assume so."

Piper added, "Wow. So Amber would have waited

until *after* the marriage with her father to murder Donna, if she did it for the money. But it seems Elias wouldn't just get more money if Donna died before the wedding, but he gets a bonus by keeping Amber, who he didn't like, from getting anything in the process. We all know they don't like each other, so it makes sense Elias might want Donna dead before remarrying for a couple of reasons. And he said in a chat room he would kill her."

Ida gasped. "Holy dollar signs. Seems Donna is worth millions. The lawyer didn't say exactly how much, but did tell Robert to make sure everything was perfect with the will because we're talking millions. With an S."

The tapping on the door was so soft I almost missed it. I raised my voice. "Come in." But instead of Dixie or Bones as expected, Edith and Lily were standing there.

"Can we talk to you?" Lily was scanning the room as she asked.

"Does everyone here think they're an employee who can just waltz right into my kitchen and office?"

"Oh hush! We know what you're doing. We might be of help." Edith smiled to let us know she wanted to be part of the group.

"And what do you think we're doing?"

Edith pointed at the laptop. "Ida takes her computer into your office. Sweetie, everyone in the house knows you are collecting info about the murder."

"Maybe, so what?"

"So, we know things that the silly computer doesn't."

"Alright. I'll give you that. Spill then."

Edith continued. "Your comments on Elias got Lily and me talking, and we remembered something. Elias was trying to start a company to build some sort of robots or something. He may have even borrowed money to start the venture."

I stared at her to make sure she knew this was important. "Edith, do you know, for sure, that he borrowed money?"

Lily replied, "Not for sure. But I saw him talking to a strange man in the general store, and overheard them talking about it. The man Elias met with was crude and even threatened him if he didn't pay back the money."

Piper interrupted, "Ginger, if Elias had large debts from a loan shark, he might've really, *really* needed money. Combine that with the timing of Donna's death *before* her marriage to Robert, and the will, there seems to be a lot of things pointing to Elias. Maybe your Aunt Mae should be told."

"You're right." I had to agree, but didn't want to revisit the police station. Aunt Mae made it clear to stay out of it, but this was a pretty juicy revelation.

"I'll go alone, it's best that way. Y'all stay here."

I wanted to get it over quick, so I briskly walked out of the pub and for a second time made my way to the police station. On entering, I could see Eunice had gone home, so I just went to Mae's desk. But before I got there, Sheriff Morrison stopped me.

"Hello Ginger. What are you doing here so late in the day? Don't you have guests to take care of at the pub?"

"I thought Mae might be working late and that she may want some dinner. I thought, maybe, we could send her something from the pub."

"I know you're poking around into the death of Donna Holland. But don't! You need to keep out of it. Understand?"

"I am. Just trying to help with some hot food from the pub. You know, keep the late night workers well fed so our police can solve the crime. By the way, you want something to eat, too?"

"No. And Ginger, read my lips – no poking around in my investigation. Got it?"

I stared at him for a second. "Ten-four Sheriff."

"By the way, Mae is not here. She is working on

something out of the office."

"Thanks for the heads up. See ya around. Sure you don't want something to eat?"

"Ginger, I'm good. And please, you and your friends need to stay out of this business. It's dangerous and we can't have you interfering with our work."

"Geeze. Auntie said almost the same thing, verbatim."

"It's because it's what we need you to do, for your own safety."

Chapter Nine

I returned to the Grumpy Chicken with a lot on my mind. It had been a long day, but my walk home provided some time to think and clear my head, just a little. It was now 7:30 and the sun had set. I enjoyed the darkness and quiet on my stroll home. Before I knew it, the main pub entrance was in front of me and on entering I could feel the air inside was thick, full of gossip and energy.

On my way over to the bar to get an update from Dixie, I felt someone grab my elbow and pull me aside. It was Beth Givens, the town gossip from the community center.

Beth smiled and said, "Ginger, I hear you've been busy today. And as I said to you earlier I would love to know more about what you saw when you found the body. Now I am hearing you have been investigating a little and you may have learned even more. We should chat?" She forced a smile, but I could tell she was slightly annoyed I wasn't telling her what I knew.

"Beth, excuse me, I'm so sorry. I have so much to do today and the pub is packed. I need to take care of my customers. We can talk later, okay?"

She took my hand in hers, and patted it gently "I will hold you to that, dear, and soon I hope!" She again forced a small smile.

Edith started to flag me down once she spotted me. "Ginger, that was quick." Lily was seated next to her, waving hello to me.

I excused myself from Beth and approached Edith and Lily sheepishly. "Mae wasn't there. But Sheriff Morrison stopped me before I could tell him anything. And he made it clear, we shouldn't get involved. So, I didn't tell him."

Lily then set her hands gently on the table, palms down. "Well, if they don't want our help, we have to do it on our own."

I sensed I was losing control of the situation. "No. The Sheriff is right, we need to leave it to the police."

Edith looked at me with a wry smile. "Deary, we know you saw a cord from a gaming system around Donna's neck."

I wanted to swear but managed to hold my tongue
– not in the dining room. "I think Piper and Ida need
to learn to be a little more discrete."

"Well, after hearing that we were thinking. What
else might be in that old den that could tell us who
murdered Donna?"

"No. I don't like where this is going."

Lily blinked at me a few times. "But, sweetie,
we're already there. You must go back and reinspect
that room for clues."

I turned red and pinched my lips. "My office, now!
I'm sorry, please?"

Lily and Edith looked at me little surprised. But
they rose and we went back to the office to find
Piper and Ida still talking and working the laptop for
information.

Piper asked as soon as I entered. "What did she
say?"

"Mae wasn't there, but the Sheriff scolded me and
told me to stay out of it. So I didn't tell him."

Edith piped up. "Ginger needs to go back to the
crime scene and find more clues."

Piper's jaw fell open. "When did you decide this."

I glared at Edith. "I didn't. Seems Edith and Lily
decided for me. After they had a chance to ponder

the headset cord I saw around Donna's neck."

Ida looked up from her screen. "Whoops. Maybe we shouldn't have mentioned that to Edith and Lily? Sorry."

I squinted at her. "No you shouldn't have."

Ida changed the subject. "Well, in the mean time I haven't found much new while you were gone. So it actually might not be a bad idea to go back and see what you can find."

"Are you crazy? That's a crime scene and the police will arrest us for sneaking back in there."

Lily added. "Ginger, sweetie, this is a small town. Things are done in a more relaxed way here. Elias is even still allowed to stay at the house. It's a big place and the police let him stay in his room if he uses the rear entrance. Just say you are going to talk to him if anyone asks?"

I stared at her, "And how would you know all that Lily?"

Lily smiled back. "Oh, dear, you know everyone out there is talking. It's harder for us not to know."

Piper jumped in. "You can't go alone. It's too dangerous. Ida and I will go with you."

"Piper, bad enough I was 'volunteered' by others to go, but now you're volunteering yourself?"

Ida added, "Well, not to be technical, but I didn't speak for myself. Piper did. I really would rather stay and do online research here."

I sighed. "Two is better than three. We not only have to avoid the police, but all those darn cats."

Piper pointed at me in an accusatory manner. "Ah ha! So you do want to go!" She recalled the pointing finger and put the hand on her chin. "And the cats, I forgot about that. Well, maybe they cleared them out to protect the crime scene?"

"One can only hope."

There was knock on the door and I groaned. "Why can't I go five minutes in my office without someone knocking on my door? That better be Bones or Dixie. If you're not an employee, go away!"

The door opened and Dog, Guardrail, and Digger were standing there.

I gasped in frustration. "What part of what I said meant come in to you?"

Guardrail shrugged, "Well, we know ya. We knew you meant come in."

Dog couldn't keep quiet. "We know you're doing something that has to do with the murder. Asking me more about Elias and his game. We want in."

"I know Amber did it and we need to just get some

evidence to show that she did it." Digger seemed to be arguing with himself.

Edith blurted out. "Well, we agree Digger. More clues are needed. That's precisely what we were talking about. Piper and Ginger are going to the crime scene to see what they can find."

I glared at the two sisters. "Edith, hush!"

Guardrail ignored me. "Well, then you'll need some lookouts, at a minimum." He pointed at Piper and me. "This is going to take more than just you two."

I folded my arms. "I haven't agreed to this dimwitted plan and y'all need to stop and think about what you're suggesting!"

Dog Breath said, "We are. We always help the police. They only have one Sheriff and two deputies. They always rely on us locals to help them."

"Mae told me the state police were coming to help. And I don't want to interfere or destroy any evidence."

Digger eagerly added. "We'll be careful. And if we find anything, we'll give it to them straight away."

I wasn't convinced. "Why would we discover anything they didn't already find?"

Lily responded. "Because you found the body and know about Elias, silly. Don't you remember? You know about his strong motives, but the police may not know that. It means something in there that seems unimportant might take on new meaning with the revelations Elias owes a lot of money to someone, and got twice as much if Donna died now and not later."

"I am not certain about this ..."

Guardrail interrupted. "I'm pretty sure the police have left the Holland house, but we should confirm that. And I have some walkie talkies at the shop we can use. The lookouts can talk to the inside people that way."

I shook my head no. "This is getting worse by the minute."

Guardrail shot back at me. "No it's not! We're forming a team."

Lily tittered. "Oh, I like that! I wish me and Edith could come and be part of the fun too. We don't get around like we used to, but maybe there is something we can still do to help."

"No, there are too many people going as it is. But thanks for offering ladies." I remembered how slow Edith was when we tailed Robert. They are in their seventies and there was no way they could do this with us. And Edith would want more free drinks for everyone afterwards.

Guardrail continued. "Ginger, you found the body,

so you know what and where to look inside. Someone should go with you to help, but who?"

Piper jumped in. "I will. I'm her best friend and it will look more natural for the two of us to be out and about together. And I can use my journalist skills to help look for clues when we're inside."

Guardrail continued. "So that means me and Dog are the eyes on the outside. And … "

Digger interrupted. "What about me?"

Dog laughed and added, "Not sure we want a grave-digger going to a murder scene, might look like you're trying to drum up business."

Digger grunted. "Everybody in here wants to be a comedian, but not a funny one of ya in the lot."

Guardrail playfully smacked Dog Breath on the back, then said. "He's right, Dog. That's not funny because everyone knows Digger would rather be drinking and eating at The Chicken than working."

Digger crumpled his face. "I give up. Why do I even hang out here."

I felt bad for Digger and shot him a friendly look. "Who is going to give you this much love?"

Digger mumbled, "If this is love, don't want to know … "

Guardrail cut him off. "Oh, alright, you can be a

lookout with us."

Ida was uncharacteristically quiet but ended her silence with, "Ginger, you got a digital camera? We should try to take pictures of anything we find. If we took something from the scene, that might be a crime. But we could take pictures and no one would know."

"No, I don't have a digital camera. But that's a good idea."

Piper threw her hands in the air. "Duh. Reporter here. I have tons of cameras. I will bring my smallest one, and my phone has a camera. Seems like the right choice for covert work."

I fretted. "I can't believe what I'm saying. This is going to actually happen, isn't it?"

Every head in the room nodded yes. Then Guardrail added, "We can be the Potter's Mill Flatfoots."

I spun to look at him. "What?"

"You know, our team. We would be like gumshoes to figure this out."

I rolled my eyes. "No, that's ridiculous."

Dog added. "How about, the Grumpy Gumshoes?"

"Don't drag the pub into this!"

Guardrail poked me on the shoulder. "Well, now

who's being grumpy."

Ida tried, "What about Team PMF. I liked Guardrail's suggestion, but it's not real catchy. Team PMF rolls off the tongue a little easier."

I looked around at everyone and said, "Are you nuts! Why are we debating this. We're talking about breaking into a crime scene and picking a team name is your concern?"

"Well, yeah. We gotta have a cool name if we're going to do this." Dog had a confused look on his face and I could tell his brain was trying to figure out why I didn't understand him.

I replied. "I'm worried we will get into trouble. Having a cool name won't get us out of jail."

"It might. You don't know it won't help." Dog was living up to his moniker. And this team name thing was his meaty bone.

I decided to placate him. "OK, what's your suggestion? And leave the pub name out of it."

Dog snapped his fingers. "How about The Festive Detectives!"

Guardrail looked up. "You know what, Ginger may be right, let's table the naming thing." He smacked his big hands together. "So now, let's gear up. We have our first stake out!"

Chapter Ten

After stopping at his shop to retrieve the hand-held radios and some other supplies, Guardrail headed for a spot not far from the Holland house. Dog Breath, Digger, Piper and I were there waiting for him at the agreed meeting spot.

Guardrail reached into the box used to carry his load and handed a radio to Piper. "You work the radio to leave Ginger free to look around for clues. You turn it on to adjust the volume with this knob. Press this button to talk, then release it to listen. And when you're finished talking you have to say 'ten-four' before you release the button to let us know you're done. Wait a minute, I meant over, you say over when you're done."

Piper huffed. "You sure?"

Guardrail scratched his head. "Okay. You don't need to be snippy, Cagney. I don't actually use these radios that often."

Dog Breath grunted then jumped in. "Maybe I

should work the radio." He snatched the radio from Guardrail. "I think I can still remember my walkie talkie codes."

I looked in the box Guardrail brought. "There are three more radios in here, just give that one to Piper, and then there are three left, one for each of you as lookouts. And if someone gets a code or two wrong, I think we can figure it out. Even better, how about we just use plain ole English."

Guardrail sulked, "Well that takes the fun out of it!"

Digger was scanning the Holland house while he talked, then said, "Let's get to the business at hand. It's a big place. We should have eyes on all four sides. So, I'll go around back, Dog can go to that far corner and watch the front and east side, and Guardrail can head over there." He pointed to a spot. "You should have a good view of the west elevation from there in the yard."

Dog nodded in agreement. "Sounds about right."

I eyed Digger and said, "It's kind of creepy you know how to stake out a place but can't cook your own meals."

Digger shrugged. "Everyone has their strengths."

Guardrail jumped in, "Looks nice and quiet, time to go. Check the radios to make sure they are all working." He reached into the box and produced a couple pairs of binoculars and some flashlights, passing the gear to the team.

Piper took a flashlight and pointed. "We'll approach from the east side, there. Then make our way round to the front door."

Dog nodded again. "Gives you the best cover, that will work."

I asked. "What if the front door is locked?"

Piper replied, "Then we go round back, or something."

Digger interjected, "If you have to go to the back door, use the east side again, less lights and has more cover."

I glanced at Digger sideways. "Again, how do you know this?"

Dog Breath didn't let Digger respond. "Alright, it's time for the Grumpy Gumshoes to roll."

I snapped at him. "That's not our name. I told you to leave the pub out of this."

Guardrail added, "I hate that name. I thought we were to be the Potter's Mill Flatfoots."

I stomped my foot. "Are you kidding me! Stop it! We don't want to draw attention and no one cares what we call ourselves. For now, we have no name."

Piper muttered under her breath, "Would be

interesting to have a secret club with a cool name."

I took a deep breath and refocused. "Look. We're about to illicitly enter a crime scene. I don't want to argue this now. Can we focus?"

Dog jumped in. "She's right." He looked to the other two men. "Time to move." Then he turned back to me and Piper. "Let's get to our posts first. Then make your move to the house." Piper and I nodded in agreement.

Guardrail, Dog and Digger told us 'good luck' and they headed out to find cover at their assigned spots. After just a couple of minutes, the radio Piper was holding squawked. It was Digger, breathing hard. "I might need some help here. There is a big black cat chasing me. Oh holy feline hell, there are more of them."

Guardrail crackled over the handset, "It's just a cat. Handle it."

Digger responded, "Is this a bad time to tell you how much I don't like cats?"

Piper pushed the button and scolded, "Get your act together, all of you!"

Dog came on, "What? I'm in position and said nothing? Don't lump me in with this nonsense."

Piper looked over to me. I was hanging my head and folded my arms. "We're going to jail, aren't we?"

Piper sighed, "I think the odds are pretty high, yeah."

The radio crackled again. "Man down! Man down!" It was Digger's voice, in a higher pitch.

Guardrail came on the radio, "Oh for land's sake, I'll go help him."

I checked my wrists. "I haven't ever been handcuffed. Wonder what it feels like."

"Oh, it isn't that bad. I was arrested at a protest in college. They use those plastic zip tie thingies most of the time now."

Dog came back on the radio, "Hey I went round back to help Digger. It's 'Nam all over again. But with cats! And crap, I think I found their dead mouse den."

I groaned. "You know we're waiting for morons to take up position to be our eyes, our only protection, while we enter and inspect a crime scene."

"I know, but we have no other choice now."

I uttered, "We should just go, we're better off without their help."

So, we made our way up to the Holland house, from the east side as planned, but without our lookouts. However, we underestimated the cats. Halfway to the front door, four cats followed almost as if volunteering to be part of our secret entry team.

Piper waved the flashlight at them. "Shoo! Git."

I noted. "Waving the flashlight around makes us visible to, like, the space station."

Piper pointed the light back at the ground. "Oh, sorry. I don't want these things following us. I even stepped on two crossing the lawn."

"Only two. I stepped on at least four or five. Crushed one's tail real bad."

Piper turned to face me. "So that was a cat. I wasn't sure if that was a cat or Digger that screeched back there." We both let out a little laugh.

We made our way to the corner of the house and I peeked around the corner to get a good view of the front door. "We need to be careful going up the porch steps, the cats like to hang out there."

"Ten-four."

I looked back over my shoulder. "You're not on the radio, you don't have to say that."

"I know, but we are on a mission and it's cool to say."

"Really? Is everyone reverting back to being ten-years old just because we're on a stake out? Come on, let's go! Follow me." I led up to the porch steps, looking for cats to avoid.

"Really! Stop that!"

I spun around. "What"

"The cats are trying to play with the light. One is even jumping up at it every now and then."

"How can anyone have so many darn cats?" I actually pondered that for a second. Donna must have owned one hundred cats. How do you even feed that many? I shook my head to re-purpose and decided to continue up the porch steps. Piper followed me.

I made it to the front door and looked back to Piper, eyes wide, then I looked back at the door knob. I reached out to check if it was locked. But before I touched the handle, the knob turned on its own and the door opened, revealing Elias. He said, "Did you have fun? You took forever to cross the lawn and I've been to rock concert's quieter than you two."

We stood still, jaws hanging. Then the radio came on, it was Guardrail. "Abort, abort! Man at front door."

Piper held the radio to her mouth. "Thanks Sherlock, I think we figured that out."

I felt like a teenager caught coming home late and stared at the ground sheepishly. "We shouldn't have come here. I know. But I found the body and thought maybe I might see something else that could help the police."

Elias pulled back a little. "Why? The police were here all day with all kinds of fancy equipment. What do you think you could do, or find, that they didn't already?

"Well, we learned a thing or two today about who might have done it."

"And who do you think did it?"

I paused, then asked, "Did you?"

Elias squinted back at me. "You know, what do you care about who killed her. No one liked her or cared what went on in this house until today."

"Well, someone killed her and is probably still in town. And we know you told your chat room friends you would kill her if she tried to remarry."

Elias grunted. "Isn't anything kept secret in this town?"

Piper promptly replied, "Nope!"

I continued, "So why did you say that?"

Elias exhaled, then took a deep breath. "Gamers sometimes try to act like the soldiers in the video games they play. You know act tough. I said that because I was mad and in the gaming world you kill the people you are mad at. It's just the way you talk as a gamer. I would never actually kill someone though. Especially Donna."

Piper went into journalist mode. "Why *especially* Donna?"

Elias' voice became a little softer, "You wouldn't believe me or understand."

Piper persisted, "It's cliche to say, but try me."

Elias took a deep breath then said, "OK, here goes. Donna and I were having an affair."

I gasped. "Good morning and good night Mrs. Robinson! Did you say you were having an affair?"

Piper murmured, "That's so gross!"

Elias shot back, "See! I told you wouldn't believe me, or understand. But it's not so hard to accept."

I cringed. "Maybe not for you. But can you try to help me understand?"

"Donna was only eight years older than me."

Piper retorted. "But she's your stepmother?"

"My dad was ancient and way older than her. She wanted someone who could make her feel young again."

Piper grabbed her stomach. "I'm sorry I asked."

Elias frowned then looked back to me. "Your friend is not helping."

I turned to Piper, "He's right, get it together,

please."

Elias repeated, "See, you didn't understand."

I looked him in the eye, searching for the truth. "I believe you, I really do, but it's the understanding that's hard."

"Donna was far too young for an old man like my father. What's so hard to understand about that?"

I replied, "Well, for starters, why did she marry him in the first place then?"

"Things were good when they first met and even for a while after getting married. But over time things changed and he paid her less and less attention. So after a while she looked elsewhere for affection."

I reached over to him and put my hand on his shoulder. "Thank you, I think I'm starting to understand."

Piper added, "Well good for you, but I am still trying to ..."

Amber suddenly appeared at the top of the stairs behind Elias and snarled. "What are you all doing here? You're not supposed to be there, it's a crime scene."

I looked up at her. "We just came out to talk. And we didn't go into the den."

Amber moved her eyes over the entrance. "Can't you see the foyer is taped off too."

I replied. "We don't mean to intrude or do anything inappropriate. We'll be going now."

Amber scowled at Elias and said, "What were you talking about with that useless lump of a man."

I answered her, "Well, let's see, for starters his step-mother was murdered today. So there seems to be plenty to talk about."

"You were talking about me weren't you? Everyone thinks I did it."

Elias turned to face Amber and said, "No, actually. They asked me if I did it."

Amber stared for a moment at Elias, then tilted her head back. "I didn't expect that. I thought everyone was still trying to find a way to blame me."

Elias admonished, "I guess we now know that's not entirely true. And I told them why I would never have killed Donna."

Amber eyed him for a moment. "So are you going to share with me why you couldn't have done it?"

Elias growled at her. "Nope. We don't share with each other, remember?"

I was uncomfortable and cut in, "We'll be going now, we don't want to intrude any further."

Amber replied, "Hang on. If you could just give me a minute, I would like to speak with you too. Elias, could we have some privacy, please?"

"Sure, I think we're pretty much done now anyway. Right ladies?" He looked at Piper and me and we nodded in agreement. Elias went up the stairs and Amber descended. As they passed, each leaned to opposite sides of the stairs, keeping the largest possible distance between them and exchanging glares with each other. Amber made it the front door and faced the two of us.

I started. "What do you want to talk about?"

"Elias. He's always been a little off, but he started acting real weird just before Donna's death. I overheard him a few times talking about starting some sort of high tech company, robots or something. And I think he borrowed a lot of money to start it."

I shrugged. "So? And why tell us?"

"Everyone knows you're poking around into the murder and you're the only one today to show me some kindness when we talked on the bench outside the police station. Plus I know you're one of the few who's probably aware I didn't do it. So you're the only one I can really tell, other than the police. And I already told them." She paused a moment. "I think he may have killed her to pay off some large debts. I don't like him at all, however I don't make accusations lightly. But he might have done it."

I reached out and touched her hand. "Thank you for sharing. I know this is hard for you."

"Yes, it is. Knowing all of this, and living under this particular roof. It is an odd situation to say the least."

Piper broke her silence. "Let us know if we can do anything else to help."

Amber nodded slightly, then started waving and bounced on her feet. "Dad! I thought you were going to spend the night there."

Robert was slowly walking up the front walk to the porch steps and replied. "I think they thought about keeping me all night. They just kept asking questions about what I was doing all day. They asked who saw me and then they would leave me alone for a while, then come back again. I even gave them all my receipts to show I was in town doing business. But they kept me sitting in the conference room, alone, until a detective finally came in and interviewed me some more, asking once more where I was all day. Finally, the Sheriff came in and told me that they weren't going to hold me for the night, so I could leave. I'm so tired now."

Amber beamed. "I was so worried. But you're home now. Are you hungry? I have some left overs in the fridge."

He smiled. "No, I'm good. And hello Ginger and Piper." We both nodded politely in reply and Robert continued. "What are you doing in the foyer. It appears to be taped off and the police told me to keep to the in-law apartment in back. We shouldn't be here."

Amber hugged her father and said, "We're pretty much done here and I was just about to head back to the apartment."

Piper added, "Thanks for the information, Amber. But we should be going now and leave you two alone. We're sorry to have bothered you."

Amber was actually smiling when she replied. "It's okay. Dad's home, things are getting better already. Oh, by the way, you should just leave using the front walk." She squinted like she was about to tell us a secret. "Less cats that way."

I laughed because she was the last person I expected to be funny. "Thanks for the tip, less cats is good. We'll see ya around. Thanks again."

We slowly made our way down the front walk. Piper whispered to me in a gruff manner. "What did she mean you probably knew she didn't do it."

"She was just guessing since she told me she didn't do it. And I do believe her."

Piper eyed me from the side of her face. "Hmph! Okay, I guess. So after all the gymnastics here, what did we learn?"

"Well, neither of them did it. But I am pretty sure

Elias and Amber are not having an affair."

Piper chuckled, "I'm surprised that they haven't killed each other yet."

And with that we went to gather our motley crew. We found Digger covered in grass and leaves, plus a foul smelling unknown substance. Dog had mysteriously applied some black makeup to his face and was shaking his right foot, trying to get all the dead mice parts off. And Guardrail had beads of sweat streaming down his face and he was breathing so hard I thought he might pass out.

I asked Dog, "Where did you get that black stuff for your face?"

Dog shrugged, "I'm surprised Guardrail and Digger didn't bring some too? It's what you do on a stake out."

I sighed.

With endless chatter about precocious cats and our failed attempt to inspect the den again, we headed back to The Grumpy Chicken while taking care to stay out of sight. While we weren't fit for human eyes, we also didn't want anyone knowing we had visited the Holland place.

It was after ten o'clock when we straggled on back to find a small crowd at the pub. We were all tired from the long day and Dog, Digger, and Guardrail went immediately for their usual stools. Piper leaned on the bar to talk with Dixie, and I went behind the bar. Guardrail plopped the box full of gear on the bar and I poured shots for the five members of the stake out team, then passed them out.

Digger spoke, "To Donna, may she rest in peace."

We all repeated 'to Donna' and downed our shots. Guardrail added, "And to the chicken, may he rest in peace and not bother us again." He took a sip from his beer after saying it. I eyed him to non-verbally let him know I didn't like mention of the ghoulish fowl in the public areas.

Dixie interrupted, "Well where is mine? Why am I being left out?"

Bones yelled through the order window, "What about me too?"

"You're both working! And "Bones you're underage." I honestly try to avoid speaking like the boss, but at times it just comes out that way.

Dixie chided me, "You're drinking, so why can't we?"

"I'm about as off duty as you can get. I'm spent. And Guardrail, please get that dirty box off the bar."

I said good night to everyone and went up the stairs to the apartment. I needed sleep and Dixie and Bones would have to close-up shop tonight.

Chapter Eleven

The next day, I woke with a headache. Discovering a murder victim, experiencing a possible grumpy chicken event in the pub, and confronting potential murderers all make for a long, tense day. But the night was even longer as I tossed and turned with no sleep. I made my morning coffee and poured an extra large mug, then carried it with me as I strolled down the stairs from the apartment to the pub.

Dixie greeted me. "What's all this junk on the bar? And are we going to talk about our chicken apparition yesterday?"

"Sorry about the mess. Guardrail must've left it there last night. And no, there is no ghost chicken, it was a fuse blowing." I stared at the filthy box. "I told him to get it off the bar. It's the stuff we needed for our stake out at the Holland place. But it wasn't much of a stake out. It turned into more of an exercise of crossing a lawn mined with cats. But we ended up having a nice visit and chat."

"And what did y'all chat about?" Dixie had a hint

of sarcasm, or maybe even jealousy, in her voice.

I took a sip of coffee. "You know, who did it. Is there still some aspirin next to the register?"

Dixie pointed at the money drawer. "Yeah, there is always a bottle there. So did you find out anything from your little chats?"

"Nope. Just got real dirty and stepped on a cat or two. And, oh yeah, Amber and Elias are not best friends."

"You know, it's not my place to say, but seems you forgot you run this place yesterday."

"I know, I'm sorry. But, I found the body and it shook me up a little. And the thought that a murderer might still be lurking among us bothers me. I know this is going to sound weird, but I need closure. I need to see the killer caught."

"Well don't forget who carried the load while you were playing Nancy Drew and stumbling around looking for a murderer. Especially when it comes time for the Christmas bonuses."

"What? When have I ever handed out bonuses?"

Dixie laughed. "Exactly. This year might be a good time to start!"

I laughed with her. She was the only person I knew who could make me feel glad to have her as my friend while asking for money. I always tried to help her when I could. It was the least I could do. She was forced to raise three kids on her own after a difficult divorce. But yesterday, she and Bones went above and beyond without me even asking.

We went to work and prepped the place, getting ready to open at eleven thirty as usual. And Bones was on time for once. Seemed today was off to a better start. But in a rare instance, our first customer was a stranger. He was big, wearing dungarees and a leather jacket with a black T-shirt underneath. He looked like a bad James Dean imitation.

He took a stool in the middle of the bar and ordered. "Give me a burger and a beer."

Dixie threw a coaster on the bar. "Welcome to The Grumpy Chicken. What kind of beer, and how do ya want your burger."

"Medium rare on the burger, and give me whatever IPA you have on tap."

Dixie nodded and answered, "Can do." She spun around and raised her eyebrows at me. It was hard to miss that this man was gruff, impatient, and most likely dangerous.

The front door opened once more and I hoped to see a friendly face. I sort of got my wish; it was Elias. He saw me and said, "Hey, how is the late night prowler this morning?"

I responded, "We didn't prowl. It was more like

loudly announcing our arrival at your place."

Elias laughed. "You're honest, if nothing else Ginger O'Mallory."

I had to say something, "Thanks, I think..."

Elias took a seat next to the thuggish man at the bar and they began to talk. As the stranger leaned on the bar and turned to address Elias, his leather jacket fell open and I saw the handgun holstered on his left side. I also heard him say, "You told me this was a sure thing."

Elias replied, "It is, it still is. The death of my stepmother has ramifications, sure, but it changes nothing between us."

"You had better be right. You know this impacts the land deal with Palmer too? Don't forget that. He wants this deal to go through. And you would be wise to avoid being the fly in his ointment. He's dealing with his own set of problems and wants this deal to go smoothly. Capiche?"

Elias looked up at the stranger, "I didn't know anyone actually said that outside of a Godfather movie, but yes I understand."

"You smart mouthing me boy?"

"No, it's just I live in a small southern town here. I never heard anyone use the word capiche in an actual sentence before."

"They said you were smart, but I don't know about that. Capiche wasn't used in a sentence. I used it in a one word question."

"I stand corrected." Elias nervously eyed the stranger for a moment. "Back on point, are we good? Nothing has changed and your boss will be paid back on time, with interest."

"I'll tell him, but if you're late, I'll be back. And I won't be happy coming back to this one horse town either."

Elias quipped, "I know, and with bells on too, I bet."

"I'll be packing, but not bells. Capiche?"

Elias nodded yes. "Yeah, capiche!"

The stranger scowled at Elias as he rose. Then he left, leaving his burger with only one bite missing and a full glass of beer. But to my surprise, Elias threw some money on the bar to cover the stranger's meal, then rose himself and chased the man out.

Dixie cleaned the bar and said, "Well that's a waste of food. And what was that all about?"

I put my hand on my chin. "I'm not sure. But did you hear that?"

Dixie joked, "Hear what. That the stranger knew some Italian lingo?"

Bones broke his long silence and yelled from the back, "You talking at me! I'm the only one here!"

I looked through the order window and blankly stared at him. "What in the world are you talking about?"

Bones shrugged, "I thought we were doing famous Italian movie lines. You know, the famous line from Taxi Driver? And what about Fuggedaboutit!"

I grimaced, "Bones, somehow those lines just don't work with your southern drawl. Just keep the kitchen caught up and clean, please."

He saluted and said, "Can do, boss. I mean yes, Godfather."

I pulled back from the order window and turned back to Dixie. "I'm surrounded by unfunny comedians." I paused for moment. "No, I was asking if you noticed the other part. Did you hear it?"

Dixie replied, "What, that Elias owes money. We know that already."

"No. Palmer. The Palmer land deal. It's the same name on that sign for the development just down the block. What do we know about Palmer Properties?"

Dixie made that weird beats me face and said, "Nothing. This is the first time I ever paid attention to the name."

"Exactly. The company is doing some major

business in Potter's Mill and no one knows who they really are. And we just learned somehow Elias is involved with Palmer. But how?"

"Oh no, the amateur detective is back." Dixie stuck her head through the takeout window. "Bones, we're going to be alone, *again*. Get ready."

I felt guilty about it, but I had to followup on this new information. "Sorry, it's just for a little while. I need to find Ida and Piper. Do you know where they are?"

"I'm not their keeper. And you're the newly anointed detective. Not me."

"Ouch. See ya in a few. Thanks Dixie." I raised my voice so Bones could hear me in the back. "Thanks Bones."

I had a new spring in my step, maybe the aspirin was kicking in. In just a few minutes, I made my way to the Potter's Mill Oracle. As expected, Piper was inside sitting at her desk, tapping on her keyboard. I burst into the office unannounced. "Hey, we got work to do. I just learned something new."

Piper popped up and motioned at the door. "Let's roll. Where are we going?"

"To find Ida. I need both of you to find out all that we can about Palmer Properties."

"Well, what happened to investigating Elias?"

"Get this, Elias and Palmer Properties may be tied together."

"How in the world did you find this out since last night?"

"Sometimes luck comes into play. And let's just say I'm glad the local pub is where everyone goes to meet."

"Ida should be at home. Maybe I can just call her?"

"Okay, track her down if you would? I'm heading back to the pub, meet me there with Ida."

I started for the The Grumpy Chicken, but stopped and turned. I headed in the opposite direction, toward the sign at the new development out near the Holland house. I wanted to reread it one more time before meeting with Ida and Piper.

I scanned the sign and realized it didn't really say much. There was no description of what was being built or who was involved. Only that something new was coming soon and brought to us by Palmer Properties. So I headed back to The Grumpy Chicken.

I arrived back at the pub to find Dog Breath, Guardrail and Digger at the bar eating lunch. I was not surprised and knew they came to discuss the recent events and what we would be doing next. Guardrail was dominating the discussion as usual, and boomed, "I told you a thousand times, we're the

Potter's Mill Flatfoots."

Digger shook his head no. "That name stinks. We should be the Grave Detectives."

Dog shot back, "What, like we investigate graves? That name makes no sense. You've worked in the cemetery too long."

I smacked the bar top with my hand. "Are you serious? With a murder to solve, you're still arguing over a stupid name for a club that doesn't even exist."

Guardrail blustered, "Well, for a group that doesn't exist, we got a lot of information on our first assignment."

I spit back at him. "Yeah, I learned Digger doesn't like cats, Dog flashed back to 'Nam with just a few cats nipping at his heels, and you left your post to go get Digger at the first sign of trouble. I wouldn't call that a team, or a club, or anything."

Guardrail looked at me sideways. "Zikes! Did someone get up on the wrong side of the bed or what?"

"Keep it up. And get your nasty box off my bar. I'm not telling you again. Next time I confiscate the box and its contents become mine!"

Guardrail knew me well enough to know I was serious. He hurriedly took the box off the bar before forgetting about it again and losing his belongings.

Just then, the front door flew open and it was Ida and Piper. Dog lit up on seeing them and said, "So, we're back in business. What's the next move for the Grumpy Gumshoes?"

I raised my voice. "Leave the pub out of this investigation stuff. Got it?"

Dog sneered, "You don't own the word grumpy, ya know."

"For this conversation, yes I do own the word and leave the pub out! If not I will own your butt too, don't try me Dog!"

Dog leaned back. "Wow, Guardrail was right, this place should be called The Grumpy Ginger today."

"Dog, you're pushing it, I'm going to …"

Ida plunked two laptops on the bar, the crashing sound interrupting everything and commanding attention. She looked around at everybody staring at her and responded, "What? We need a place to set up, get things really humming. I brought the needed laptops and necessary peripherals."

I asked, "And why does this have to happen here?"

Guardrail didn't miss a beat. "Because we got the brand spanking new whiteboard here." Dog and Digger laughed at his comment.

I sensed I was being too hard on everyone and tried to find a centered calm voice. "The whiteboard is for pub business only, got it."

Dog laughed and said, "Yeah. Just like we had buffalo wings yesterday, wink, wink."

I threw my hands in the air. "I give up. So Ida, what are you really planning?"

She pawed through the wires she also brought while she answered. "I thought of a few things we should explore further. And last night while you were out I set up some web crawlers, a kind of data mining program to get more information on our list of suspects."

"I don't know what that is, but sounds like it might get us more information?"

Ida never looked up but said, "One can only hope!"

Piper jumped in, "So, what's our next move?"

Dog couldn't resist. "Pick our name?"

Even Guardrail flinched and all of us just decided to ignore Dog Breath for now. I said, "Palmer Properties. We need to learn all we can about them. They have more to do with this than we thought."

Piper noted, "The name on the letterhead?"

I pointed at her. "Correct. The one and the same. Who are they, what are they doing in town, and are they working with Elias Holland."

Ida finally looked up. "What? You think Elias and

this Palmer Properties are connected?"

"Maybe, but that bit of info stays here. Capiche?"

Dixie started laughing at me and said, "OMG! You hear one person say it today and now you're repeating it."

"I liked when they used it in The Godfather, like Elias said. Guess the comments we heard earlier stayed with me."

Digger had been quiet but looked up and asked, "What is this Ka Fish thing? Is it something new on the menu?

Dixie was laughing even harder now and replied, "Sure Digger, you can have the first plate made."

Digger got excited. "It's on the house too if it's the first plate, right Ginger?"

I couldn't resist so I said, "Sure. One plate of Ka Fish for Digger today, on the house."

From the grill in back, Bones bellowed, "I'll make him an order of Ka Fish he can't refuse. Fuggedaboutit!"

Chapter Twelve

Ida took over my office and set up a small computer center. Then she went to work looking for information on Palmer Properties. I walked back to the dining room to chat some more with the rest of the gang.

I saw Edith and Lily, earlier than usual, at their table and I knew they were here to be part of the team too. So I went over to them and took a seat.

Edith greeted me with, "Good morning dear! I hear we need to knit you a ski mask."

I scrunched my face. "What?"

"We heard about your late night antics. You need some help with your covert operations from the version of the story we heard."

"I forgot. I don't know why this town has a newspaper, we don't need one. Everyone knows everything about what goes on here. And faster than a high speed internet connection."

There was no lunch rush today and the place was empty, and very quiet. Piper heard me and sat up, protesting, "You know why we need a paper. What gets passed around town so fast is gossip, not news."

I clarified, "Sorry. I'm glad we have a newspaper and we need it, so don't be offended Piper. I was just making a point."

Piper got up from the bar and came over to sit at the table with us. "Apology accepted. But don't be surprised if you hear a retaliatory remark aimed at the pub from me before the end of the day."

"I deserve that, I guess."

Edith was all business today and ignored our chatter. She got right to business. "So, what are we going to do next?"

Lily answered her. "I think we need to dig a little more on that unpleasant Amber girl."

I couldn't hold back anymore. "I have something to tell you. Don't be mad. When I was at the police station yesterday, I learned that Amber has an airtight alibi. She didn't do it. I'm sure."

Piper said, "You little busybody! How did you find that out and not tell us?"

"Amber told me she didn't do it. And the police let her go right away. It was kind of obvious. But I thought I would let the police do their job and see if they really did clear her."

Piper sulked. "Well, what else are you holding back?"

"Nothing. I promise. It was something Amber told me in confidence and I honored her privacy. But it just seems like the right time to tell y'all"

Lily jumped back in. "Well, that makes Elias suspect number one then, if we rule out Amber."

I sighed. "Well, no. He didn't do it either. We learned last night he was having an affair with Donna. He lost some inheritance money if she remarried, yes, but he was still well off and he had no reason to want her dead."

Edith huffed. "Well, we're running out of suspects, sweetie."

"No, there is a new one that has emerged this morning. Palmer Properties, the name I saw on the letter in the den. Ida is checking them out right now."

Edith asked, "Aren't they the ones developing that site not too far from here?"

I nodded, "The one and same."

Ida came out from the back and sat at the ladies table. She plunked herself down like a sack of potatoes. "Well, if things aren't strange enough already, seems like from what I've found so far, Palmer has ties to the mob."

Piper asked, "You need to pick your words more carefully. Mob can can mean multiple things. Like those flash mobs we see in viral videos for example."

"OK, Miss Merriam-Webster, I meant mob as in the Sopranos."

I gulped, "And we had some good fella at the bar this morning first thing. What's going on here?"

Dixie came over and took a seat. "What's going on girls? Saw the gossip circle, and it's dead in here, so I had to join."

Edith answered her. "I'm not sure, dear, but from the silly chatter going on it seems we got a Sopranos problem now."

Dixie nodded, "Yeah, you heard about that armed guy saying capiche at the bar then."

Ida jumped in, "Dixie, I don't know for sure about the guy you're talking about. But I do know we're talking real world mob ties to Palmer Properties."

Dixie's face went white. "Moldy mozzarella! I served a wise guy this morning?"

Ida smiled, "Maybe, and he's most likely from New York from what I see."

Edith shook her head. "Our poor little Potter's Mill, touched by organized crime from New York? Unbelievable."

I had a different question cross my mind. "Why would they want Donna dead though?"

Ida stared at me blankly. "I don't know. From what I can see, her death might actually be a problem for them. But I need more time to dig up some dirt."

I looked at her like I was staring over the top of imaginary glasses, "Then why are you out here? Sounds like you have some computer work to do."

"Gee-sh! I'm not one of your employees you know. Guess I shouldn't have updated anyone and just kept the new information to myself." And with that Ida rose and stomped back to her computers.

I shouted after her. "I'm sorry, good work. Let us know if you find anything else."

Ida never turned or slowed and quickly disappeared through the door into the kitchen on her way to the office. I couldn't help myself and said, "She may not be an employee, but she handles the swinging door better than Bones."

Lily interjected, "Oh, pish posh. Ida does have a job to do as part of our team. She volunteered to help, so let her stew. She'll figure it out and she will be fine."

I lamented, "Why does everyone keep calling us a team?"

Edith immediately responded, "Because we are, and a good one at that. Look at what we have learned in less than one day."

Lily held a lone finger to her lips, and went,

"Shhhh!"

I spun around to see Guardrail, Dog, and Digger approaching our gossip circle. I asked, "Why are telling us to hush? If we're a team, they're definitely members."

Unfortunately, Dog heard the word team and he beamed. He held his arms up like he was giving us a big air hug. "The Grumpy Gumshoes at work!"

I hung my head in defeat and said, "Not this again."

Guardrail added, "She's right Dog, we have other things to discuss. What are you gals talking about?"

Piper replied, "Seems Elias and Amber are not very good suspects. But I think you know that already. However, we learned that Elias may have ties to Palmer Properties. And Palmer Properties may have ties to organized crime."

Dog asked, "What like Al Capone?"

Piper nodded, "Exactly."

Digger chuckled and added, "They better pay their taxes, that's how they got Capone you know?"

I cut them off. "Thanks for the history lesson, but can we stay focused on Palmer Properties?"

Dog perked up and smacked Guardrail on the back. "Hey, I might have been right! It's a professional hit man *from the mob*. See, they're the only ones who like to use cords like that to choke their victims."

Lily jumped in. "Boys, can you do something for us?"

Guardrail answered, "Sure, we're members of the Potter's Mill Flatfoots."

Lily waved her hand in the air. "Whatever we're called, I don't care. But we need to have you go to town hall and look up the permits for that development project being done down the block from here. The one by Palmer Properties. But do it quietly. OK?"

Dog stroked his gray pony tail like he did when he was thinking, then added, "Sure, but Bones used to date the clerk down at town hall. You should send him, he can get whatever you need."

I couldn't believe I didn't think of it. "Sure, that's a good idea. I'll work the grill and send Bones."

Ida reemerged from the back office. She looked like she had news. "I just got scolded by the FBI!"

I shot to my feet at hearing her announcement. "What? On my network?"

"Oh, don't be so dramatic. It was a posted message on one of the Palmer sites. But seems the FBI has lowered the boom on them. Confiscated some of their sites. I am guessing Palmer is looking to team up with people like Elias to use them as fronts."

Piper started thinking out loud. "So Elias may not be as innocent as we think. And the mob wouldn't hesitate to dispose of one small town black widow if it suited their needs."

I added, "I'm going to send Bones down to town hall to get the names of all those involved with that project. What else do we need?"

Digger raised his eyebrows. "A little luck. If the mob is involved, we should be careful."

I sighed, "Now I understand why Aunt Mae was so adamant about staying out of this. She and the Sheriff told me this was dangerous."

Guardrail threw in, "Let's stay positive. For now nothing really changes and let's see what names are associated with that development project."

I rose and said, "Alright, lets wait for Bones to complete his errand." Then I left for the kitchen to take over the cooking and sent Bones on his way.

Chapter Thirteen

Bones returned after about one hour and held a piece of paper as he came through the front door. I came out of the kitchen as everyone gathered at Edith and Lily's table to hear the latest news. So I went to join the group.

Bones waved the paper. "Made a copy of the permit, was easier that way. There's not much in the file for that project since it hasn't started construction yet." He slapped the paper down on the table.

I asked, "Well, what about the plans, or paperwork needed to get the permit?"

Bones held up empty hands. "Wasn't anything. The permit is for the sign. Everything else is pending."

Digger said, "Well, that was a bust."

Bones smiled, "Not a complete bust, I started chatting with Abby and she's giving me another chance. Got another date with her while I was there."

Digger shook his head, "To be young again."

I picked up the paper and read the permit. I saw Donna Holland was listed as the property owner and that she held the title. "Do you think Donna loaned Elias this piece of land? Seems she owns it free and clear. She might have tried to help him?"

Lily asked, "Then why did he take loans?"

"The property is just one piece. He would still need to construct a building and install equipment, hire people, get supply lines, all kinds of stuff that requires money."

Edith asked, "Why didn't Elias just ask Donna for the money? She was loaded, right?"

I raised my eyebrows. "That's a good question. And did we mention that last night Elias admitted he and Donna were having an affair."

Edith and Lily leaned back and fanned their faces. Edith gasped and muttered, "Oh my, I think I have the vapors. This is awful. How could she do that? The horrors that house has seen!"

Lily added, "Maybe Elias did it precisely because they were lovers. You know the lover is always the first suspect."

I jumped in, "No, I think Elias didn't have cause. He needed her to help with his business. And when he talked about her, it seemed like he genuinely cared about her."

"But you don't know that." Dog stared at me to underline his point.

I nodded back at him. "You're right. But I know someone who might know how they got along...Amber."

Guardrail said, "Amber goes from suspect to informant in less than twenty-four hours, is that a record?"

I continued. "But it makes sense. She doesn't like Elias, at all. She didn't even want to be on the stairs with him last night. If she has dirt on him, she will spill it. I should go and talk with her again, alone."

Piper said, "I can go with you if you want?"

"No, I should go alone. She opened up to me at the police station. I think she is more comfortable one on one."

"Alright, but be careful. We still don't know who to trust."

"I know, but it would be useful to know if Elias and Donna were fighting."

I saw Bones head back in the kitchen to work the grill. Business was still surprisingly light today. It seemed the big day yesterday took its toll on more than just me. But I was glad, it meant Dixie and Bones would get a break, at least till dinner, because I needed to head back out to the Holland house.

"Dixie, you got the helm, again!"

She saluted navy style. "Aye, aye, captain."

I headed out the front door, and once again was on my way to the Holland house. I usually got my exercise scurrying to and from tables with dinner plates and mugs, but the last two days I was burning up the town sidewalks. I arrived at my destination after about fifteen minutes to see Amber sitting on the porch, drinking tea.

I waved as I walked up the front walk. "Hello, how are you this morn…" I wasn't looking where I was going and tripped over Harry Potter. I landed on my face in a not so elegant fashion.

Amber jumped up. "Oh my gosh! Are you alright?" She ran down the front walk to help me get up.

"I'm fine, but I should know better. I've been here enough the last two days to know to watch for cats."

"Thank goodness most of them are outside cats. I don't why Donna wanted so many?"

"That's funny, I thought the same thing last night."

Amber helped brush me off then looked me in the eye and asked, "So why are you here?"

I paused at her directness. "Honest answer? Because I know you didn't do it. But you might know something that can help us find out who did."

"The police already questioned me extensively and I told them everything I know."

"Then it won't hurt to answer the couple of questions I have."

Amber recomposed herself and continued. "Would

you like some tea? And maybe I can get a wet cloth to clean your hands. Is that blood on that hand." She pointed to my right side.

"Wow, look at that. Just a little scuff. But some tea and a wet cloth would be welcome right about now."

"Take a seat on the porch and I will get them for you."

"Thanks."

Amber went inside to get the tea and wet cloth. I stepped up onto the porch and took a seat next to the one she was sitting in. Gypsy recognized me and came over to rub on my leg. Then she jumped up into my lap and I scratched her ears. She purred so loud that she seemed to vibrate in my lap.

Amber returned with a tray and set it down on a little white table between the chairs. She handed me a wet cloth and eyed Gypsy in my lap. "I see you have a friend. That's surprising, that cat doesn't like anybody. I guess I was right to trust you. Gypsy knows it too."

"Thanks. But my relationship with Gypsy is a lot simpler than you think. The cat has been mooching off my pub for years. She just likes me because she gets some food out of the deal."

"I don't know, I can hear her purring from here and you don't have food for her right now." Amber paused a moment and took a sip of her tea. In a teasing voice, she asked, "So, more to the point, why are you here? Again!"

I was a bit taken back by her sense of humor. "I know it's a little weird to be here after last night. But I was surprised to learn Elias and Donna were having an affair. Did you know?"

"Yes, and I told my father. He didn't seem to care. Said he just wanted companionship in his old age and if she wanted an open marriage that was fine with him." Amber shrugged. "So it seemed there was no talking him out of it, even though I kept trying. I knew Donna's reputation as a black widow and I was still afraid she might pull something with my father. I was frightened for him even if he wasn't."

"I appreciate that, but I need to ask you something. It may be important. Did Donna and Elias argue, even a little?"

"No, that's one reason I kept quiet about it. They actually got along very well and it made both of them happy."

My jaw suddenly fell open. "I can be so stupid. You and Elias hate each other because your father was to marry Donna. But you didn't know if the affair would continue – and Elias was afraid the affair would end."

"Duh, of course. It seems Donna runs through men like they're shirts that you just change when you get tired of them. Plus all of her older husbands seem to end up dead. Not the kind of woman I hoped to see with my father. At best, I figured she would keep her boy toy Elias. Not a great situation for my father to marry into."

"I get it, *now*. I guess it is hard sometimes to really appreciate what someone else is going through."

"Thanks, I appreciate that. It's hard to go through this alone. Kind of nice to able to talk to another woman about it." She readjusted her tea cup. "So why are you so interested in them now."

"Because, we have a murderer among us and they need to be caught. We're a small town and we take care of our own."

"I'm from Atlanta, it's not like that there. We tend to just let the police do their job."

"I know. And I hope you can forgive us for waiting to properly welcome you to our small town. It takes time for the locals here to accept outsiders"

Amber plunked her hands down into her lap. "I understand and it would have been just fine if not for Donna's murder. But after she turned up dead, everyone immediately assumed it was me because I was an outsider. Even the police. That was just too much with everything else I was dealing with and I should have kept my composure a little better. But that is water over the bridge now."

"I feel terrible you had to deal with those issues

alone, at least your father is here with you. Please, let me know if I can do anything to help. I feel so awful about how this happened."

"Thank you. You're the only one to actually talk with me, like a friend. I really do appreciate that."

"You're more than welcome. This tea is real good." I took one last long sip. "But I should be going now. I have a business to run. You should come on by, hang out with everyone."

Amber smiled. "I think I will just keep to myself till this all blows over, thanks."

"Well, if you change your mind, I owe ya a drink in return, so your first one is on the house."

"Thanks, but you won't make much money if you give away the drinks."

"It's the least I can do. You know, a kind of small welcome gift."

Amber laughed. "Thanks."

Robert emerged out of the front door, looking formal in a suit and tie. "Good morning ladies, fine day to be alive."

I smiled at him and said, "Yes it is. But I wish Donna was here to enjoy it with us."

Amber grumbled, "I don't want to talk about her or the murder if that's okay."

Robert patted her shoulder. "It's alright, dear. We need to be going anyway. Amber and I have business to attend to and apologize for cutting this visit short."

I stood. "That's fine. I was just leaving anyway. I have a business to attend to myself. Thank you for the tea and hospitality." I nodded to both of them and navigated my way around the cats as I walked down the front walk.

I left feeling guilty. Amber must have experienced loneliness and fear with the death of Donna. Edith and I thought she was a little unhinged when we saw her outside the crime scene. But I realized she was pretty composed after learning of the Elias and Donna affair.

My walk back was a blur as my mind was lost in thought. Before I knew it, I stood in front of The Grumpy Chicken. I entered and saw business had picked up. Seemed the town was coming to life again, but I saw the Edith and Lily table was empty and the boy's regular bar stools were vacant. I guessed that Guardrail, Dog, and Digger went back to work and Edith and Lily were likely making their daily rounds of the Main Street stores.

Dixie was humming behind the bar making drinks. "Hey, look who's back. Bones and me were starting to wonder if you got lost. Maybe you even forgot where the place was."

"You're in a good mood. What happened? You get

a date with a millionaire GQ model or something?"

"Nope, not that good. Elias came back just after you left and paid his bar tab from yesterday. He apologized for forgetting about it and squared up, plus a big tip. You might want to know what he told me too"

I chuckled. "So you want to play detective too?"

Dixie winked at me oddly. "Who better. Bartenders get dumped on with all kinds of personal stuff."

"So, what did Elias tell you?"

"He has an airtight alibi. Was at the waffle place with Johnnie Gilbert. He drank coffee and played with his phone, chatting when Johnnie had to work the grill and couldn't talk to him. The police confirmed it with Johnnie and Elias said they would confirm it with his phone records too."

"Holy digital! Of course, phone records. I didn't think of that. Where did Piper go?"

Dixie snorted. "Are you kidding? After hearing Elias has an alibi, everyone is going nuts trying come up with a new suspect list. Everyone is in your office now, arguing."

Chapter Fourteen

I scurried through the swinging door into the kitchen and made a beeline for my office. But I was stopped short. The whiteboard on the wall was now full of writing. On the left side was a list of people with percentages scribbled in beside their name. To the right of each name was a comment, that clearly was a list of possible motives for each person.

I burst into my office to see Ida at my desk working furiously on her keyboard. Lily and Edith were sitting on five gallon pails and Dog, Digger and Guardrail were arguing while playing with the soft tip darts in my office. I demanded, "Who used the whiteboard for non-pub business?"

Edith looked at me puzzled. "Why, all of us of course, dear."

I eyed Dog. "And is that your handwriting for all those percentages written next to the names?"

Dog flinched. "What, can't I contribute?"

I growled, "No, not like that. That could be considered gaming. I can't have that associated with the pub. You need to erase all of it, now! And I mean erase it so it is completely gone, no shadows!"

Piper put her hand on my shoulder. "Ginger, we're just trying to help. You don't have to be so hard on us."

"I don't want to lose my business, so no I'm not being too hard on you." I paused, then continued, "But I'm sorry, Dog, if I was a little terse."

Dog squinted at me. "Terse? Funny word. But seems about right. Apology accepted. I'll go erase it. I don't want to hurt you or the chicken." He left to do the chore.

My voice shrank a little, "Thanks. So what else did you find while I was gone. Seems Elias has a good alibi."

Ida looked up from her screen. "Yeah. And I am trying to double check his phone records."

I was afraid to ask my next question. "Is that legal?"

Ida chuckled. "Well, no. You must have heard about all the hullabaloo about the government collecting metadata on cell phones. It's a touchy subject. But phone records are just another database that can be accessed."

"Um, what does that mean Ida. I don't want the FBI showing up here."

"Don't worry, I covered my tracks really well and no one can trace what I'm doing."

I pleaded, "It's not that I doubt your abilities. We all know you're good. It's just what we don't know all the ways the government can track us. They always keep the best tools secret so you can't be sure they're unable to track you. I don't want to do anything illegal here that they can find."

Ida shot back, "Well, too late. I just found his records."

I tilted my head back in resignation. "SON of a chain gang! I'm just trying to get sent to jail this week!"

Ida touched her chin. "I just used your network, so technically, it was accessed from my laptop and I would be the one to go to jail."

Guardrail piped up, "See, you worry too much. Ida has it covered. Now we need to figure out who could have done this, we're out of suspects."

Digger objected, "No, Ida may have overlooked something with her logic. We could still be accessories to the hacking crime, maybe."

Guardrail punched Digger in the arm. "Quiet, you're not helping."

Edith held her hand up. "Now, now. And stop with the Punch and Judy tactics Guardrail. Let's be civil. We've pretty much ruled out Amber and Elias now. They were our two best suspects. But the third was Silus Palmer, of Palmer Properties. Seems we need to give him a harder look."

Lily added, "They're out of Savannah. And Silus is pretty well known there."

I asked, "How do we learn more about him? And where was he yesterday morning?"

Ida answered. "Already did. I checked his email and he had a busy schedule all day yesterday in Savannah. Hard to confirm if he attended all the meetings on his schedule, but I am working on it."

Digger added, "Well if Dog is right, a guy like him could have hired a hit man, right?"

I looked to Edith and Lily. "That would mean a stranger would have come into town and murdered Donna. Then they would have had to make a get away. Is that possible without being seen?"

Edith answered me. "It was broad daylight. Would've been real hard, especially with the Holland place not far from the strip on Main Street. But I guess it's possible. And maybe they didn't make a get away because they're still here, hiding."

I nodded. "I agree. Dog's theory may be more credible now." I could hear him scrubbing the whiteboard, but the commotion stopped.

Dog stuck his head in the office door. "See, ya should listen to me more." Then he went back to work.

I turned my attention back to Ida. "This phone records thing with Elias has me thinking. This is a small town. Is it possible to determine who was on the cell towers yesterday around the time of the murder?"

Ida exhaled like a popped balloon. "You thought hacking Elias' individual phone records was too dangerous. So you don't want to even discuss trying to access the towers and everyone who was on them yesterday morning."

Then a new idea fluttered through my head like a butterfly and I couldn't ignore it. "What about this? I go talk to Elias and just ask him about Palmer. He might know something and be willing to tell us."

Piper added, "I think Elias is back at the waffle place again. Seems he's friends with Johnnie, but he is really spending so much time there because he has a crush on the new waitress there."

I grabbed her wrist, "Come with me and I want you in journalist mode when we talk to Elias."

The gang watched as Piper and I left. We made our

way across the street and headed straight to the waffle place. Potter's Mill had three good lunch and dinner spots, including The Grumpy Chicken, but breakfast belonged to Johnnie Gilbert and his waffle place.

We entered to see Elias sitting at the counter talking with Johnnie. We took the stools on either side of him.

Elias smiled. "Well, the night prowlers."

I tried to use my most contrite voice. "We're sorry about last night, honest. But now we were hoping you could answer a couple of questions for us. The developer helping to build the business you wanted to start, Palmer Properties, is an unknown to us. Can you tell us a little about him?"

Elias' smile faded. "You just don't give up, do ya? Alright. Donna did some work with him in Savannah and suggested him when I started going forward with my robotics business. The operation was going to need some space, so she agreed to develop the lot out near the house and build the office slash manufacturing slash warehouse I would need."

I shrugged, "That all sounds pretty straightforward, so why bring in a developer?"

"Well, it required contractors, and some specialized equipment. Silus Palmer has connections and he agreed to help Donna make the contacts. He even sent a letter to her with all the people to call.

Silus never came out to Potter's Mill or did anything beyond that. Oh, except the sign. I went down to the town hall with the paperwork Donna gave me for the sign. Silus had filled out some forms, or something, to have his name listed as the developer. Donna felt it would help get the contractors on board if they saw Palmer's name. That's it. Well one more thing, Donna did say that Silus may get some kickbacks from the contractors he recommended. So there was a little money in it for him too."

Johnnie had gone back to working his kitchen but came out to the counter. "Look at this young man! Flirting with my waitress all the time, now he has two pretty ladies sitting on either side of him. Some guys have all the luck."

Elias laughed. "I'm not sure you want these two surrounding you, Johnnie. They have bad habits like sneaking up on your house in the middle of the night. And they ask ALOT of questions."

Johnnie chuckled, "I heard about that! Is it true, did the cats take down Digger?"

Piper broke her silence, "Look, we were just trying to help the police find a murderer. Maybe we pushed it a little too far last night. Maybe. But I'm not going to apologize for caring about who killed Donna. And yes, Digger was accosted by some kitties."

Elias rolled his eyes. "Well, after all these questions and having some fun at Digger's expense, are we done?"

I jumped back in, "No, one more question. Did you see anything out of the ordinary yesterday, a stranger or unusual car?"

Elias nodded his head no and raised his eyebrows, "No, not that I recall."

Piper then asked, "I know you think we're being nosy, but did you give your phone to the police?"

He turned to look her in the eyes. "How did you know that?"

"Just a guess. You mentioned to Dixie that your phone records would show you were here yesterday morning. Easiest way to do that is check the phone itself."

Elias said, "Yeah, I need to get a new one as a matter of fact. They told me they might keep my old phone for a while."

Johnnie's look turned serious, "I have to be honest, all this checking alibis and the murder yesterday, it just doesn't feel right in our small town."

I pinched my lips then said, "That is well said Johnnie, and I agree. We apologize for intruding and thanks for the chat."

I rose and Piper followed my lead. We left silent till we were on the sidewalk.

Once outside, Piper looked at me from the side of her face. "What was that all about? And why did you end the our conversation so quickly?"

"It's pretty obvious Silus Palmer was doing Donna a favor. They may have done some business in the past and seemed to be friendly. But it just doesn't add up that over a project where only a sign was erected, with no other money exchanged, someone would be driven to murder. And Elias confirmed Silus was trying to help by supplying contacts and using his name to bring in the needed contractors. Easy money for Silus to just let them use his name and do nothing else. If it went bad, what exposure or loss does Palmer suffer, nothing. Silus Palmer had little motive to kill Donna."

Piper chuckled, "Sometimes we think alike. I had the same thought, but I was going to ask a few more questions to confirm it. You said you wanted journalist mode, you should have let me work."

"No time, we should get back to make sure Digger and Dog haven't turned my pub into a gambling hall or Ida hasn't hacked the pentagon."

Piper stopped and looked me in the eye. "If Ida checked Elias' phone records, why can't she check Silus, and everyone else we suspect?"

"Like you said, sometimes we think alike, it's why I wanted to head back."

She smiled at me and we crossed the street with a new sense of urgency. We burst back into the office and Ida was working alone. The rest of the crew had gone back to doing their business as normal.

I asked, "Can you check the phones for Amber, Silus Palmer, and Robert too?

Ida shrugged, "Sure, will just take some time."

I knew I would regret it, but I said, "Do it."

Ida went back to her screen and keyboard. Piper looked at me weird and asked, "Don't you think the police already did that? And why add Robert?"

"We have pretty much ruled out Amber and Elias. Silus Palmer just doesn't add up. So we have to go back to the beginning. And the lover is always suspect number one."

The door to the office opened revealing Lily and Edith. Lily said, "We saw you come back, what did you learn?" She closed the door behind her.

"That Silus Palmer is not a good suspect. He has no real motive and likely has an alibi."

Edith asked, "So where does that leave us? We're out of suspects!"

"No, we are checking the phones for Amber and Silus Palmer to confirm what we have learned. But I also want to see the phone records for Robert Harlow."

Edith's face went white and Lily whined. Edith finally said, "We saw him doing his business as normal yesterday, and he didn't look guilty at all. Remember? Plus, the police found he was in town all morning, seen by multiple people. How could he be a suspect?"

Lily added, "And he has very dreamy eyes."

The office door flew open once again. This time it was Digger and Dog. Dog Breath said in a defensive tone, "What are we missing?"

Lily answered, "That Piper and Ginger have lost their minds. They want to start checking Robert again."

Digger asked. "So, why is that a big deal."

Edith said, "It's silly! He's such a gentleman. How could someone who dresses so nicely do something so dastardly like murder Donna? And he wouldn't get a dime till he married her, so he had no motive to kill her till they were hitched. And most important, he has an alibi."

Digger replied, "Maybe it's him, or his daughter. I still think we ruled her out too fast. Why can't it be a girl?"

Guardrail burst into the already overcrowded office, "What did I miss?"

Dog rolled his eyes, "I just asked that!"

Guardrail added, "And?"

Digger tried to help. "Ginger wants to look at Robert again. But Lily thinks she's lost her mind."

Guardrail chuckled. "Well, Ginger may have lost her mind, but that's nothing new. So, what happened to the Palmer developer guy?"

I answered, "Didn't pan out. Looks like he has an alibi. And there is no motive for him."

Guardrail folded his arms, "So we don't know squat is what you're saying."

Piper answered him, "That's one way to put it, albeit not fit for print. But sums it it up about right."

I hung my head. "I can't believe I'm going to say this. But Dog, can you recreate what was on the whiteboard, minus the percentages? I repeat minus the percentages."

Dog flinched his shoulders. "Sure, should be pretty easy. I have it pretty much memorized."

Digger piped up. "So what are you saying, we are starting over"

I uttered, "Exactly."

After a few minutes Dog came back into the office and proudly announced, "All done."

Guardrail jumped on him, "I better check, you get things mixed up sometimes." He pushed Dog out the door so they could review what was written.

Lily rose, "I want to see too."

And then everyone spilled out into the kitchen, just outside my office to gawk at the whiteboard.

Digger summarized, "Four suspects, and one motive that seems to repeat, money."

I added, "No, Elias could have been jealous or angry about the upcoming marriage of Donna to Robert. And fear could have driven Amber in an attempt to protect her father. Dog add those to the list. And we have no real motive for Palmer, other than some money that might get kicked back to him. And money might be a motive for Robert, but he wouldn't receive an inheritance till he actually married Donna."

Lily protested, "Why is Robert even on the list? He is so kind and gentle. And he was seen in town. It doesn't make sense. And as you just said, he had no reason to do such a terrible thing. Thank goodness he didn't marry that awful woman."

I answered, "Glad to see you and Edith are keeping your emotions out of this." I waited a moment to let the sarcasm in my voice sink in along with the point to the spinster sisters that we needed to use logic, not emotions. Then I continued, "Beth is such a gossip, but she said something interesting just after the murder. The lover is always suspect number one. And Lily, you said to suspect the lover when you thought it was Elias. Why not look at Robert too?"

Dog raised his voice, "I still think it's a pro. I'm telling ya, hit men are the only ones who kill so clean, with no blood."

Digger challenged him, "Why do you keep bringing that up. I don't think we have assassins running around in Potter's Mill."

I agreed, "It would be hard for a stranger to come into town in broad daylight and not be seen. But if you knew what you were doing or had some help, maybe. But there are other problems with that theory. Someone would still have to hire him, and for what reason? That brings you back to our list of four. The motive would have to be pretty strong to hire a hit man. But a strong motive does not seem to exist for any of them."

Piper said, "You know, seeing this all up on the board, it looks to me like Robert, Amber, Elias, and Silus are our most likely suspects. In two days, we found no others to add to that list. But we did pretty much rule out all four. What if the assumed time of murder is off, then the alibis may not be as strong as they seem. That brings Amber, Elias and Robert back into the discussion."

Lily raised her voice. "Oh for heaven's sake, I can't believe we are back to this silly notion where Robert is on the list."

I added, "It's not silly if he did it. Maybe there is a motive we just haven't found yet."

Piper agreed and yelled back to the office. "Ida, you got anything on Robert yet?"

Ida answered, "Nope, will take some time. But I did set up some additional web crawlers. They take even more time."

I was exhausted and said, "Alright, seems Ida's little electronic bug crawler things, or whatever you call them, need time. So let's regroup tomorrow just before the street fair. We can check what we find from the phone records and anything else she finds online. And in the meantime, maybe we'll think of something else to investigate."

I heard Dixie came through the swinging door into the kitchen and stride on back to join the discussion. She asked, "What did I miss?"

Dog leaned over and whispered to Dixie, "It was a hit man."

Dixie ignored Dog and insisted, "Well? Anything new."

Lily blurted it out, "Everyone has gone mad and thinks we have eliminated all our suspects. So we have gone back to suspecting everyone."

Dixie shot me a glance and said, "Good grief, when it comes to suspects for Donna's murder, you guys bounce around more than a kangaroo on a trampoline."

Dog spun to Dixie, "I would love to see that, can

you imagine."

Piper's voice took a condescending tone and she hung her head. "And with that, rational discussion dies a horrible death."

I added, "Piper's right, we're all tired and we're pretty much done for today. We should regroup here tomorrow morning just before the street fair for the art gallery opening. Agreed?"

Everyone nodded yes. We were all tired but I needed to push myself to close the night out. So I went to help Dixie and Bones finish with the dinner crowd and the group in my office dispersed. Most of the gang went home, except Dog Breath and Guardrail who went to their usual bar stools for one last beer. There was an uneasy air to it all as we went into waiting mode for some unknown electronic thingy to find information for us.

Chapter Fifteen

Potter's Mill is a small town and the last thing you would expect to find is a fine art gallery. But three sisters, Cathy Douglas, Blanche Diaz, and Janis Bishop, believe they can make a profit selling art here. The grand opening was scheduled for today and the whole town pitched in to celebrate the ribbon cutting by throwing a street fair to coincide with their first day of business.

It was early and even though the last two days were long and hectic, I couldn't sleep and rose early with one question nipping at my brain. Who murdered Donna? I couldn't ignore it, so I finished my morning routine and wandered down from the apartment over the pub.

Upon strolling into the kitchen, I saw the whiteboard and took another look. I couldn't help but wonder who or what we missed and more questions flooded my consciousness. Only four suspects, are there others? Three seem to have strong alibis, but can we really rule them out? Who had a motive strong enough to warrant murder? And did Ida get us all in trouble?

The last two days flew past and I was tired. People

get things wrong when exhausted and I wanted to avoid missing something or making a mistake. Working with Piper and the gang helped minimize the fear of missing something, but not completely. I went into the office and sat at my desk. Scanning the screens, I saw text scrolling from top to bottom at a rapid rate and felt stupid for not knowing what I was looking at.

I heard a familiar voice bellow, "Boss, your first mate reporting for duty!" Dixie had arrived and must have seen the lights on in my office.

I yelled back, "I'm in here!"

Dixie made her way into the office and took a seat. She looked at me like she wasn't sure what to say. "You look tired, the ghosts keep you up all night?"

Mention of the grumpy chicken might have been a mistake because the lights flickered in response to her comment. And it seemed impossible, but the next thing we heard sounded like a chicken clucking, "Evil!"

We heard a loud crackling similar to electricity arcing and the lights went wild for a few seconds. Then everything returned to normal.

My eyes were wide and I knew my skin was white. "Dixie, maybe you shouldn't ever mention our namesake mascot...like ever again."

Dixie's eyes were even wider and she was looking

around like she might find something else. "What the feathers? That was real creepy. What was it? And don't tell me another fuse!"

I tried to keep my voice steady. "Maybe it was a fuse. Let's go have a look." I looked down at the laptop screen and what I saw stopped me from rising. On the screen, the scrolling text now flowed around some odd blank spaces. And those blank spaces formed two letters – R and H. I finally realized what I was seeing and did not want to spook Dixie. I continued to stare at the screen and said, "Let's go check the fuse box."

"Okay. But I'm not touching anything in that electrical box. Two incidents in about two days, it may not be safe."

We went into kitchen with the intent of moving over to the corner where the fuse box was mounted. But we stopped just outside the office. The whiteboard was now damaged, with a shallow dent like someone had punched it. And the ink colors changed. Most of the letters had faded to a light gray almost too light to see. Except for two words – Robert and secret. Robert was in a faded red that bordered on pink. And the word secret was in the middle of the dent, glowing in bright green. I felt my knees weaken.

Dixie broke the silence. "You can't ignore this. That board was not like that two minutes ago. It had to be the chicken. You heard the clucking voice that said 'evil'. And this? It had to be..." She leaned over to me and whispered. "It had to be our ornery fowl."

In a rare instance, I was speechless. Dixie clearly heard the same thing I had and these changes on the whiteboard were impossible. The green glow of the word secret was not natural and nobody else was in the kitchen. How could this happen?

Dixie whispered again. "Our paranormal clucker is trying to tell us something."

I rebutted, "There has to be an explanation. Someone may be messing with us. I'm checking the fuses." And I went to check the electrical box, but nothing was wrong and no fuses had burned out.

The rear door of the kitchen opened revealing another impossible occurrence...Bones arrived early to work. He eyed the two of us. "You both look like you've seen a ghost."

Dixie blurted back at him. "Don't say that. You don't know how right you are."

I needed to move past the unexplained event to the business of the day. "Look, it's weird, yes. But we have work to do to get ready for the fair. The tables need to be set up out front. And don't forget the white tablecloths. We want it to look nice."

Dixie gave me the side eye. "So we're going to ignore all this?"

"For now. What else can we do. Best thing to do is get back to normal as fast as possible."

Bones chuckled like a surfer that just rode the perfect wave. "Whoa, look at the way that one word is glowing green."

I grabbed his shoulders, turned him toward the hanging aprons, and pushed him in that direction. "The whiteboard is unimportant right now. We need to set up!"

Suddenly we heard a loud knock at the back door and we all jumped. Bones answered and Piper entered with Ida. We all stared at the two of them and Piper defensively said, "What?"

Dixie chortled, "You don't want to know."

I added, "She's right. It's been a weird morning and we need to set up for the fair. But I would like to talk with Ida in my office for a minute, alone."

Everyone knew I was leery of Ida's hacking and that I thought she could be difficult to be around sometimes. So my request drew odd looks ranging from surprise to shock. Ida nodded and we went into the office and I shut the door.

I told her, "Look at the screen. What could have done that?"

Ida took a seat at the desk and threw her hands in the air. "Look at what? My crawlers are doing their work like they should."

I moved around the desk so I could see the screen. The text was scrolling down the monitor as usual but the 'R' and 'H' blank spaces the text had been flowing around were gone. I was stunned but did not want to let Ida know. "Oh, alright. I didn't know if all that fast scrolling was normal." I was bad at stalling so I added, "Then can you tell me if your automated stalkers found anything?"

Piper entered uninvited, but I knew she decided we had enough time alone and she did not like being left out. Ida continued pecking at the keys a few times and looked up. "Elias phone records do show he was at the waffle place like he said. And Amber was at the realty office, per her alibi. Silus, I don't know, still don't have all the information. And Robert? Nope, still nothing on his phone records either. Robert is older, he might not use his cell phone much."

"Okay, thanks." I left Piper and Ida in the office and went to back to work. This murder business was starting to frustrate me and I needed to do something normal, to take my mind off of it. I opened the cardboard box and inspected the huckleberry wine plus some unusual liquors made from the same fruit. I decided to exhibit and sell unusual huckleberry drinks in front of the pub as our part in the street fair. Dixie wanted us to also include some moonshine, but I had to be careful not to flaunt the Georgia alcohol laws. The huckleberry concoctions were the perfect compromise.

I heard the front door in the dining room open and the deep voice boomed through the order window into the kitchen. It was so loud it almost hurt my ears. "The one and only Guardrail reporting for service."

I faintly heard Dog's voice scold him. "You don't need to announce yourself like the King of England."

The front door opened and closed once more and I assumed it was Digger who was always not far behind Guardrail and Dog. I told everyone to show up early, and they did.

I moved out into the dining room to greet the boys. "How are the grumpy braindeads?"

Dog mumbled, "You don't have to be mean about us wanting to have a cool name."

Guardrail ignored Dog and asked, "Did we learn anything new?"

"Kind of. Ida's creepy little electronic stalkers found that Elias and Amber were telling the truth. They both have strong alibis. Robert and Silus, we're still waiting on their records."

Dog chimed in, "So all of our suspects are out?"

I answered, "Well, really two are out. Robert and Silus haven't been ruled 'out,' but they don't seem to have a good motive for murder."

Digger shook his head. "Edith and Lily are not going to want to hear that. They think Robert should be ruled out."

I sighed. "Well, Lily and Edith need to see past their emotions. And if you think about it, it's pretty much where we left off last night, only a little more sure about ruling out Amber and Elias."

Dixie became animated and added, "What...you aren't going to spill? Tell them about the whiteboard!"

"Shhhhhh!" I held my index finger to my lips as I hushed her.

Dog was master of the obvious and said, "So what happened with the whiteboard?"

I surrendered, "Go see for yourself." As I expected, the strange transformation of the whiteboard generated large amounts of unfocused energy in the three men.

They came back into the dining room and Guardrail looked skeptical. He sneered, "Alright, who's the wise guy. It had to be Ginger or Piper. You two have been pointing toward Robert since yesterday afternoon. Well, we're smarter than that and won't fall for your tricks. But who punched the board? And how did you get that one word to glow green like that? It's kind of cool."

I responded, "You're right. We shouldn't fall for tricks. Look we have the street fair to set up for, and I could use your help. Give us a hand with the tables and we'll talk more about it later."

Dog always liked being part of the pub functions and jumped into the kitchen to help Bones. Digger went back outside for some unknown reason, and Guardrail just stared at me. He eyed me and said, "So what really happened?"

"Nothing!" I didn't need this distraction right now.

Dixie for some reason seemed to think I needed help to expand on my one word answer. "You don't want to know and we can't tell you anyway. Might cause something else weird to happen."

Guardrail turned to look at Dixie and scrunched up his face. "Umm...that made no sense."

Dixie winked at him and said in a low tone, "Big guy, trust me on this one."

The front door opened and it was Edith followed by Lily. They had some photos with them, which I had asked to borrow to show how the pub looked years ago as part of our exhibit at the fair.

The swinging door to the kitchen opened and out came Dog carrying the box of huckleberry liquors. He made his way to the front door and on seeing the two spinsters, he volunteered, "Good morning ladies! Not much new this morning. Still looks like Robert did it."

Lily stammered. "Oh, poo! He is too well refined to be a murderer."

Though I wished different, Dixie spoke again. "Well our whiteboard says different." Lily just looked back at her confused. So Dixie added, "Go have a look for yourself."

Edith and Lily took her suggestion and went into the kitchen to view the whiteboard. After a couple of minutes, they emerged back into the dining room and Lily spoke before even getting to her table to sit. "You didn't have to resort to such extravagant measures to point at Robert. That was very immature of you Ginger."

I emphasized, "I didn't do anything."

Edith politely asked, "Fine, dear, but you're not fooling us. So is there anything else we can do to help set up for the fair?"

Lily added, "By the way, dear, how did you get the ink to glow green like that?"

I threw my hands in the air. "I didn't change a thing on the whiteboard, so I have no idea why the green ink is glowing. For now, can we get back to setting up for the fair? We need to get glasses and the mobile register set up outside. Dixie, can you please get that done?" Finally, my efforts to focus on the fair paid off and we began to get the tables and chairs out on the sidewalk.

The town took pride in its street fairs, and as usual, a banner was hung over Main Street right in the middle of the strip. We all focused on the sidewalk to get set up so The Grumpy Chicken could contribute. Dixie organized one table as an order pick-up station with the register and another for taking orders and displaying the wares. Lily and Edith then left to wander around the shops once outside, while Piper and Ida continued the internet searching in my office. For the next hour or so the boys helped finish the set up for the fair, running extension cords, bringing out ice, whatever was needed; they were my unofficial employees in times like this. As a finishing touch, I brought out an over sized, framed menu so passersby could scan our food selections in hopes they would stop and buy some lunch. As I adjusted the pictures loaned to me by Edith, smoothed the linen tablecloths and arranged all the liquors on display one last time, I noticed Ida had left the office to poke her head out the front door. She looked concerned and flagged me to come over to her.

I complied with her request and once I was standing next her, Ida looked around to see who might overhear what she was about to say. When she was happy we were isolated enough to talk, she whispered, "I found something we should have known by now. But get this, Robert and Donna eloped last week."

I smacked my forehead. "Ginger Nicole O'Mallory, you foolish girl! How could I be so dumb."

Ida just stared at me. "Why are you mad at yourself?"

"Amber was real upset just outside the crime scene. She even seemed to be mad at Robert. If she knew they just got married, she knew he would be suspect number one. Her reaction was telling us that they were recently married if I just paid attention. And if Robert married Donna, he would be in line for a large inheritance if she died. That's a motive."

Ida hushed me, and whispered, "Not so loud. But we know now, so what do we do?"

"This is big, I have tell Aunt Mae. Everything is pointing to Robert. This is a blockbuster. Are you sure about this?"

"Sure. I found the marriage certificate in Savannah. Seems everyone thought they went to Savannah about ten days ago to do some business there, but they were eloping and got married there."

"I need you to keep looking for Robert's phone records. Would it help speed up the search if we just focus on him?"

"Sure, I can turn off all the other searches. But do we really want to do that?"

"Yes. But we can discuss our options with Piper too if it makes you feel better."

Ida chuckled. "She is in your office right now scolding herself a lot harder than you did. She can't believe she missed it either. And she told me to ask you what we should do next."

"Like I said, we tell Mae. The police need to know this."

"Okay, but you got a lot going on with this fair today. You want me to go find Mae?"

"No. I need to do it. We're family and it will be easier for me to tell her."

Chapter Sixteen

It was now mid-afternoon and I tried my Aunt Mae's cell phone, twice, but she didn't answer. So I needed help to find Deputy Owens fast. I heard Guardrail, Dog Breath, and Digger bickering as usual in the kitchen. I think it was something about why chlorophyll made leaves and grass green and not some other color. After the whiteboard incident, it seemed everyone was obsessed with the color green. I moved into the kitchen with them and chose to just ignore their bantering to get to the point. "Gentlemen, I need your help finding my Aunt Mae. It's real important that we find her and I have to speak with her, right now."

Guardrail replied, "Gentlemen? That must mean you really need us. But it shouldn't be too hard. The fair means everyone will be hanging out on Main Street. But why don't you just call her?"

I replied, "I did, she didn't answer. Mae is investigating the murder and who knows what she is digging into and where she is. But I *really* need you to find her. Oh and by the way, if you come across the Sheriff, don't tell him what you're doing. Okay? He's not too keen about our efforts to help with the investigation." All three of them nodded and headed out to find Mae.

I needed to search too, but first I went back to the sidewalk out front and checked our tables to make sure we were up and running and contributing to the fair. Then I scanned the nearby area, looking for Edith and Lily. The two spinsters were likely perusing Main Street to inspect the various booths and stations of the fair. I spotted their neatly groomed gray hair across the street talking to Velma Harris who runs the local sandwich shop.

I crossed the street and they saw me coming. They finished with Velma and started slowly down the sidewalk to meet me. Edith was smiling and said, "What a beautiful day for a fair. The art in the new place is, let's say, unusual. I'm not sure who would buy paintings like that with all those weird images and colors, but they sure have a lovely day for the first day of business."

I didn't want to appear too desperate so I let her finish with the snipe. Then I said, "Ladies, I need your help."

Lily perked up, "Oooo, must have something to do with the murder. Is there news? We were just on our way to the pub to see if Ida found anything else."

"Yeah, there's news. Robert and Donna eloped last week. So they were married at the time of her murder. I need to find my Aunt Mae and let her know. This means Robert stands to inherit Donna's money, and with the amount of money involved, he might have a strong motive to want her dead."

Lily gasped, "Oh my, I can't believe he actually put a ring on the black widow."

I added, "Yeah, Robert may not be the proper gentleman you think he is."

Edith sputtered, "That's impossible!"

"He married Donna for sure. Ida found the marriage certificate."

Lily shook her head no. "Well that's just terrible news. I'm so disappointed."

I felt bad for the two ladies. They were genuinely shocked and Lily clearly had a crush on the man. "Please, I need your help to find my Aunt Mae. She needs to know so the police can use this information."

Edith took a reassuring tone. "I'm so displeased, but we will help you, dear. You know we will always help you."

"Thank you. Can you ladies look in the shops on this side of the street?"

"Sure."

"And if you run into the Sheriff, don't let him know what you're doing or what you know. He wants us to stay out of this and will be mad if he thinks we're messing in his investigation. But this is an important piece of information that I need to get to Aunt Mae."

"We know. And the Sheriff is at the fair, dear. We saw him earlier; he looked tired. We'll tell him nothing about what we've found."

"Thank you. I have the boys looking for Aunt Mae too, so we have multiple teams looking. We should be able to find her pretty quick. Let me know immediately if you do find her. Call me on my cell phone."

"Will do, dear."

I left to head for the police station. The boys and spinsters were checking the shops on Main Street. But the best place to look for a deputy was in her office at the police station. So I went to cover that base.

But first, I started back to The Grumpy Chicken to tell Dixie and Piper where I was going. However, I stopped short of my intended destination to see Guardrail, Dog Breath, and Digger talking with Star. No one knows what her real name is, but she runs the New Age shop next to the pub. Star was dressed in a tie died dress and outfitted with all sorts of costume jewelry. She was tiny and she looked pretty. The boys loved to be around her but they were never brave enough to actually go into her store. Things in the shop like crystal balls and tarot cards were just too strange for them. So it seemed that they took the rare opportunity to talk with the mystic outside on the sidewalk where it was safe. The only problem with that is they were chatting away the time instead of searching for my aunt.

I made my way over to them and approached from behind. "Eh-hem! I thought you boys had a job to do?"

Guardrail spun around, "Ginger! We're looking. But we just took a little time to speak with Star."

"That's nice. But did you forget, I need to find Mae, now?"

Digger added, "Like Guardrail said, we're looking. Just in our own way."

"Well, I need you check all the shops, not just Star's. Okay?"

I folded my arms and watched as they said their good day's to Star. Then they moved on down the sidewalk. I looked across the street to see Lily and Edith checking the art store.

Star asked, "How have you been Ginger?"

"Good, thanks for asking. You?"

"Fine. I know those boys would never be seen in my shop, but you should come by sometime for a crystal ball reading."

"I might just do that. But right now I need to find my Aunt Mae. Have you seen her?"

"Early this morning. Saw her leave with a bag of donuts and cup of coffee from the waffle place."

"Thanks, Star. I don't mean to be rude, but I need to get going. I need to find my aunt. If you see Mae, can you let her know I'm looking for her?"

Star nodded, "Sure."

I smiled and waved goodbye to Star stopped to tell Ida and Piper what was going on and that I was headed to the police station. Then I headed out and made my way down the sidewalk. After only a couple of minutes, though, I threw my head back and moaned. The boys had stopped again. This time they were outside Grandma's Diner, eating and talking to the owner, Mable Mirth. Mable had set up a substantial food service area in front of the old time diner and it was already pretty crowded.

I scurried over to them for a second time. "Are you serious?"

Guardrail slumped at the sound of my voice. He spun around and replied with a full mouth. "A man's got to eat. And come on, we don't always have deep fried gator being sold on the street."

Dog was trying to finish his corn dog without me seeing it, but didn't do a very good job of hiding it. Then he gagged as he tried to eat it too fast. I asked him, "Did you swallow the stick?"

Guardrail slapped him on the back and Dog spit out

the offending bit on the sidewalk. Dog looked up at his big friend and said, "Did you have to hit me so hard?"

Guardrail shrugged, "Have it your way. Next time I'll just let you choke."

"If you didn't get sidetracked and just did what you're supposed to be doing, no one would be choking. We need to find my aunt, now. Please?"

Digger tried to respond but nothing beyond grunts and growls came out since his mouth was full with barbecue sandwich. I put my hands on my hips and must have had a stern look on my face because all three took that as a sign to leave and continue searching.

Then I spotted Lily and Edith sitting on a bench outside the general store. They were under the large green awning that covers the front windows eating ice cream from the cart set up out front of the shop. I rushed over to them and said, "I thought you ladies would be more focused than the boys. Why are you sitting on a bench eating worthless calories and not out looking for Mae?"

Lily didn't look up but replied. "But, sweetie, we are looking. We're just looking smart. We're in our seventies, remember, and we can't scurry around on the sidewalks like crazy women." She then eyed me to let me know they had at least seen me making the rounds. "And we can see most of Main Street from here. So why not enjoy a little ice cream while we stand vigil?"

I exhaled the air in my lungs followed by a new refreshing breath, then continued. "And have you seen her?"

"No. We would have called you if we did."

I pointed out, "Then maybe this isn't as good a method to look for Mae as you think?"

Edith patted the seat next to her. "Deary, relax a little. You're too worked up this afternoon. I think this murder investigation is getting to you. I haven't seen you this bossy since your divorce."

At that moment, Sheriff Morrison walked up and stopped next to me. He leaned on one of the thick black painted lamp posts lining Main Street, causing the large ornate glass shade mounted on top to wobble a bit. He addressed us in his official, deep voice, "Hello ladies. I am sure we're just talking about the street fair, and nothing else. Am I right?"

I sheepishly replied, "Yes, of course."

He tipped his hat to the elderly sisters. "Good. Let's keep it that way."

I nodded and said, "Ten-four. Message received loud and clear."

Sheriff Morrison walked off slowly and looked back at me over this shoulder once with a glaring look to emphasize how serious he was.

After he was out of earshot, I continued, "Why does the Sheriff just show up at my side but I can't find my own aunt? I tried her phone a number of times but just got her voice mail. So now I need to go down to the police station to see if she's there. Please, can you two make the rounds and check the fair again to see if Mae is here while I go down to the station? We need to find her now. Alright?"

"And we're helping, dear. We'll find her."

"Thank you." Edith was right, I was a little worked up running back and forth on Main Street strip hunting for Aunt Mae. So I took another deep breath and refocused. I gave a weak wave goodbye to the two sisters who were still working on their ice cream and set out off the police station.

I made it to the facility and went inside to find Eunice on the phone. She waved hello to me then held up an index finger. So I waited a minute. Eunice finished her call, hung up and said, "Are you looking for Mae?"

"Yep. Is she here?"

"No. But that was her on the phone. She had something to check out in Savannah, but she is on her way back. I told her you were here and she suggested you wait for her on the bench outside. You timing is good, she should be here in just a few minutes."

I said thanks and went outside to take a seat. And

just like Eunice said, it wasn't long before Aunt Mae returned to one of the parking spots out front. She was driving the lone police car owned by the town. Mae got out carrying a cardboard box that looked to be full of files. She plunked the box with a thud on the end of the bench then took a seat next to me. She put her arm around my shoulders giving me a kind of side hug and said, "Ginger, always so nice to see you. How were the buffalo wings the other night?"

"We had a change of plans. I didn't make them."

She sat up straight. "Oh, that's too bad. Well, I hear you've been looking for me. What's up?"

"We learned something you should know. It may help with the murder investigation and you're the only one I can tell."

"Sugar, I told you to stay out of this. But alright, what is so important that you have to come down here to tell me?"

"I had to come down here. You weren't answering your phone.

Mae sighed. "I've been so busy with the murder, calling all over the state, chasing files and information. Sorry, honey. But I did see you called and was planning on coming by the pub later. But seems you couldn't wait."

"This won't wait. Donna and Robert eloped. They got married last week."

Mae stared at me blankly while faintly shaking her head side to side. She finally said, "This is a dangerous thing you are messing with, honey. You need to let the police handle this. And Ginger, dear, I already know that. Got a copy of the marriage certificate in that file box right there. Just retrieved a fresh copy of it and interviewed the clerk that filled it out." She pointed to the box on the end of the bench. "So see, leave it to us and let us do our job. I have a lot to do right now, but see you later sweetie." Mae kissed me on the cheek and collected her file box. Then she entered the police station and went back to work, leaving me alone and embarrassed on the bench.

Chapter Seventeen

I took a brief respite on the bench outside the police station by folding my arms, throwing my head back, and closing my eyes. I was tired and humiliated that Mae already knew about Robert and Donna. In theory, I did the right thing telling her. But after thinking about it, I should have known the police would find out about their marriage. I was being silly to think we were helping.

I wondered about everything that transpired, including the weird occurrences in the pub. What did the 'R' floating on the green brining chicken wings mean? And what were those strange blank spaces that formed 'R' and 'H' on the computer screen right after the second time the lights went funny? Were these references to Robert Harlow? And the whiteboard highlighted his name seemingly on its own. How could that be? And the word 'secret' also appeared, glowing green in a weird dent. Could that mean their elopement was a secret, leaving Robert in line to inherit a large amount of money? Was the grumpy chicken really trying to tell me it was Robert?

Was I losing my mind? I've heard every story there is to tell about the chicken ghost while growing up. But could the tales be real? And was all this to just to tell me something? Or was it really the fuse box and I own a business that is getting ready to have an electrical fire?

Then my phone rang. It was Ida and she was talking fast. I had to stop her and request that she start over. She repeated, more slowly this time. "I found a plane ticket out of Savannah! Robert has a plane ticket out of the country to the Cayman Islands. It looks like he is planning to run."

"Crap! He's trying to Juliane Asange us! We have to keep him from leaving. I'm still at the police station, so I'll tell Mae. When is he supposed to leave?"

"Later tonight! He has a flight from Savannah to Charlotte, where he connects to the islands."

"Get everyone back to the pub. I'll be there shortly after I tell Aunt Mae. I'll see ya then!." And I hung up before either of us could say goodbye.

I sprinted back into the police station and I came in

so fast it made poor Eunice jump as I blew past her on my way to Aunt Mae. I stopped just short of her desk and tried to catch my breath. I stammered, "Robert is running. He has a ticket to the Cayman Islands. And he's leaving from Savannah later tonight."

Mae looked up, eyes wide. "Well there's a barn burner that I didn't know. How did you find this little nugget of knowledge? And are you sure?"

"Ida found it and we're sure. For now, please don't ask me about how she found it. More important, if Robert is trying to run we have to stop him."

"I agree. But with the murder investigation and the street fair today, our force is spread thin. The Sheriff and Deputy Wise are working the event, but I think we should pull the Sheriff off that duty to help."

"Whatever we do, we need to move fast. We don't have much time."

"Let me call him." Mae pressed the talk button on her radio mic and called the Sheriff. "Kelly, glad I got you. Listen, Ginger tells me that they found a plane ticket for Robert Harlow to the Cayman Islands. And he is scheduled to leave today. Seems like we need to check it out and stop him if we can."

Mae put her hand on the small ear bud to hear better and nodded her head a couple of times, then said, "I understand. I will take care of this then. No problem. We were talking about bringing him in again anyway."

I was dialing my phone. Guardrail answered. "Listen, I may need you to help us keep Robert from leaving. He has a plane ticket to get out of the country."

Guardrail used his best tough guy voice but it didn't work because he was chomping on some other food from the fair while he spoke. "I already heard from Ida. Me and the fellas are ready to help with anything he might try, even if things get rough. If you know what I mean."

"I'm not sure what to expect, but we don't need any heroics. Can you get back to the pub to be with Ida and Piper and be able to roll at a moment's notice?" He agreed and I continued, "Good. With the fair and murder investigation our Sheriff and deputies are pretty busy. You might have to be my cavalry today. Thanks." I hung up.

Mae was waiting for me to finish. She said, "The best place to start is the Holland place. But we're on our own. The Sheriff is already at the fair, so he is going to look for Robert there in the event he went down to there like everyone else. We should go and check the house now before Robert gets wind that we know about his plane ticket. Does anyone else know about this?"

"No. Well maybe. Guardrail did know so maybe Ida told some others."

Aunt Mae grabbed her hat and put it on, adjusted it just right, then said, "We better move then! Lets do this."

We loaded into the car and made the short drive over to the Holland house. Aunt Mae parked out front and we both popped out of the car.

Mae held up her hand and said, "Whoa, Missy. Where do you think you're going?"

"To help you."

"Nooooooo, you wait here. This could be dangerous. Stay here."

I snapped back, "But you can't go up there alone."

"Yes I can. I'm trained for this, but you're not. You watch my back from here and if something happens, you call for help and stay out of sight. Unless I tell you different, I don't want you leaving the cruiser. Got it?"

I nodded yes and added, "Good luck!"

She smiled reassuringly and turned to head up the cat infested front walk. I knew Aunt Mae my entire life, but I was seeing her in a new light now. She had one hand on her holstered weapon and needed to watch the house for danger while moving up the sidewalk with all those pesky cats around her feet. She was far more graceful than I had been the last time I used this front entrance. And I wasn't chasing a potential murderer when I fell over a cat making that same walk.

Aunt Mae made it up the porch stairs to the front door and knocked. I was surprised at how hard and loud she rapped on the door, but if anyone was in there it would be hard to miss.

The door opened and I saw Elias. Aunt Mae talked to him for a short period, then she sprinted to the car, hurdling a couple of cats on the way. When she was about ten yards from the car she shouted, "He's at Daryl's place, doing some last minute business with Amber! Get in the car, we need to move quick. Elias said he had packed bags and took his golf clubs too. He's definitely on the move!"

I reverted to a ten year girl and bellowed, "Oh my gosh, I can't believe this is happening!" I jumped into the cruiser and buckled up.

Mae did the same, flicked on the lights but kept the siren off. Then she put it in gear and sped off for the realty office. Normally, it would have been a ten or fifteen minute walk, and it should have been a two minute car ride, but the fair made it harder. We arrived via back roads and parked in the rear on River Street as most of Main Street was blocked to traffic.

Mae jumped out and ordered, "Same rules as at the Holland house, stay with the car!" Then she cautiously approached the realty office run by Daryl Reid. As Aunt Mae made it to the back door of the office, I saw Edith and Lily coming down the alley road between the realty office and the sandwich shop. I fluttered my hand in the air to flag them down and they slowly made their way to the police car. I got out and stood next to the car waiting for them. At that point, I saw Mae greeted at the door by Daryl and she entered the office. Lily and Edith took a minute, but finally made it over to me. I asked, "Did you see Robert at the fair?"

Lily answered, "If he was there I would have seen him. But he wasn't. Funny, Sheriff Morrison asked us the same thing again."

I pointed to the building and said, "We think he is in the realty office, but we're not sure."

In response to my last comment, Aunt Mae emerged, chatting with Daryl. Seemed she just poked her head in to take a quick look. They shook hands and she moved back to the car. Aunt Mae threw her hat through the car window and clicked her talk button once again. "Kelly, he's not at Daryl's place. Daryl says he was there earlier, but left to pick up some special order items at the general store. Did you see him over there?" She paused. "Really? I have the cruiser and will head back out to the Holland place." Mae clicked off and shot me a look over the roof of the car. "Let's go!"

I almost swore. "Crap, I should call Ida, have her keep an eye on his travel plans."

Edith piped up, "Ginger, we'll tell her, ask her to try and track the status of the plane ticket. Ida might even be able to cancel his reservation. We got it covered. Go find Robert."

I jumped into the car and before I snapped the buckle in tight Mae floored it. She kept her eyes on the road while she talked. "Amber was with him. Robert told Daryl that after picking up some stuff at the general store he was heading out to Donnie Freeman's garage. Amber was going to drop him off to get one of Donnie's rental cars. Then he planned to drive out to the Savannah airport. Kelly is going to head over to the Freeman garage with Deputy Wise and he told me to get over to the Holland house in case they head back there for some reason. At a minimum, Amber should be coming back to the house and we want to talk to her too."

Then my phone rang. I answered and heard Guardrail's voice. "Ginger, Edith told me you're running around ragged with Mae. I'm heading over to my shop to pick up my motorcycle. It's fast and can get around town easier with the street fair going on. I can help you, but where do you need me to be?"

"I'm not sure. Believe it or not, we're heading out to the Holland place again, but Sheriff Morrison might need some help at Donnie Freeman's place."

Mae took one hand off the wheel and started waving at me. "NO! I don't want you or your friends getting involved anymore than you already are."

"Um, Guardrail. I'm not sure we need you to do

anything right now, so stay put with Ida and Piper at the pub for now. I need to go and will call back if we need something. I gotta go." I hung up.

Mae put both hands back on the wheel. "Good girl. This is getting out of control. I wish we still had those state and federal guys here to help. They show up for doughnuts, but when we need some real work done, they're back at their cushy offices."

"Wow! That's as close to a mean thing as I've heard you say Auntie."

She glanced over to me quickly and added, "This thing isn't over yet. You might hear me say something far worse before it is." And at that point, she locked up the brakes and we skidded to a halt in the same place in front of the Holland house that we had just left a few minutes earlier.

I stayed in the car and Mae made a hasty exit. She didn't even bother to put her hat on. Once again she made her way up the walk, but halfway, she froze. After a few seconds, she turned and headed back down the front walk. She got back in the car and looked white. She said, "There are two cars on the side of the house. One I think is Robert's and the other looks like one of Donnie's rentals. I think they both came back to the house." Mae clicked her talk button, "Kelly, I got two cars here. It's possible that they both came back here. You find anything?" She listened for a moment. "I think you should get out here then. I'm alone with no backup." She nodded slightly and said, "Thanks."

I asked, "Well, are we going to just sit here?"

"For a few minutes. The Sheriff confirmed Robert did pick up one of Donnie's rentals, but he left already. So a suspected murderer might be in that house with potential hostages. I need backup. And Sheriff Morrison is on the way." Mae scanned the road. "With all this traffic for the fair, I wish I could block off the roads, darn it."

"I got that covered." I picked up my phone and called Guardrail. "Hey! Listen, I need you and Dog over at the Holland place, with some help if possible, to shut down the roads around the house. And I need you here quick. ... Thanks."

Mae was giving me the stink eye. "Ginger, can you tell me when you went deaf? Because you don't seem to hear anything I tell you anymore. They really need to stay out of this."

"Blocking the roads is safe, easy work they can do while staying out of your way. They can at least do that to keep other innocent people away from this, from maybe getting hurt."

"I hate to say it. But with the fair going on just down the road, blocking off the roads around here would help. I wish we had a bigger force. Kelly did say he would have Deputy Wise with him, so we should be in good shape if Guardrail can block off the roads. Let's hope nothing happens at the fair because we'll have all three of the Potter's Mill police officers here in a few minutes."

We waited for a few minutes, watching the house for signs of movement. Mae decided to quietly move the car to block the driveway and just as she was about to park, we heard it. Loud rumbling of motorcycle engines. Our attempt to stay quiet was for naught. Guardrail and Dog appeared on their motorcycles, each with riders on the back. And to my surprise, Edith and Lily were the ones riding shotgun.

Chapter Eighteen

Guardrail and Dog parked their bikes next to the cruiser, smiling ear to ear. Lily and Edith were also smiling and their gray hair was unkempt, making them look wild and, well, different. I rolled the window down and Guardrail asked, "Where do you want us?"

I greeted them with, "Why didn't you bring Digger?"

"The cats, he doesn't like 'em. And Lily and Edith wanted to come." He was looking at the house as he spoke to me.

Mae cut us off, "We need to keep civilians away from here till we have the situation under control. Can you shut down Main Street out here and divert traffic while we move to take any suspects we find into custody?"

Guardrail snorted, "Suspects? That sounds so official."

Mae glared back at him, "It is. Do what you need to in order to divert people from this place, that's all. Nothing more, got it? And stay out of our way. No one is to to do anything stupid or interfere with police business."

Dog Breath raised his eyebrows, "Wow! Never seen you so official and commanding, Mae. That's hot in a woman."

I flinched. "Dog, sometimes you need to keep your fleeting thoughts to yourself. I think you need to go now and direct the traffic."

Edith and Lily were fixing their hair and giggling like little girls. Edith prattled, "I haven't been on a motorcycle for weeks."

Lily shot back, "Oh, don't exaggerate, it's been longer than that. But I have to admit I still love the exhilaration of riding on the back of a hog."

Guardrail shivered and said, "That just sounds weird coming from Lily."

Mae raised her voice. "Are y'all done being teenagers? You have a job to do! Let's get to it!"

Dog stood straight. "Yes ma'am!" He had a silly smile on his face, which didn't help the awkward moment.

Guardrail grabbed him by the scruff of the neck and said, "Come on soldier, you're with me. We got traffic duty. You too, ladies, I want …" His voice trailed off as they walked out to the middle of the road to set up a traffic detour.

Mae had rested her noggin back on the headrest.

"This is the team you've been poking around the murder investigation with? I'm surprised no one's got hurt yet."

I smiled. "Well, Digger did get taken down by the cats."

Mae chuckled. "I heard about that this morning when I bought my breakfast at the waffle place. But you know what really bothers me, you found the plane ticket, not us, with a crew like that."

"Technically, Guardrail or Dog didn't find the plane ticket, Ida did. She's pretty good on the computer."

"And how much of what she did was illegal."

"Can I plead the fifth?"

Mae eyed me sternly and we were spared further uncomfortable discussion about Ida's techniques when Sheriff Morrison showed up with the only other deputy Potter's Mill employed. Mae got out and met them at his civilian car. She gave him a summary of the situation and the Sheriff replied, "Deputy Wise, you head around back to cover the rear. Deputy Owens, I need you to watch my back here in the front. I'll approach the front door to determine who is inside and try to talk them out of the building. Simple plan but let's be careful. We have no idea who is here or how violent they might be."

Deputy Wise headed round back and Deputy Owens, my normally kind Aunt Mae, drew her side arm and held it at her side. Sheriff Morrison made his way up the front walk and when he encountered a cat, he simply prodded it out of the way. I wondered why I hadn't thought of that.

Mae whispered to me through the window. "Can you call Ida, see if she found anything else about the plane ticket? He may have changed his plans. It would explain why he came back here."

I dialed the phone and made the request. For some reason Piper answered Ida's phone and she told me nothing had changed. She promised to call back with anything new. I informed Mae and I saw her nod to confirm she heard me, but she stood firm using the cruiser as cover and never took her eyes off the front of the house.

The Sheriff knocked on the door and I held my breath. But to my surprise nothing happened. Mae's posture was taunt, almost nervous looking, and I heard her mutter, "Come on, answer the door." Then Mae got her answer, but it wasn't what she expected. She put her hand to her ear and exclaimed, "We got a problem!"

Sheriff Morrison sprinted down the front stairs and around the side of the house. He moved fast and Mae sprinted up the front walk and followed him. Apparently someone was trying to leave from the rear of the building.

I got out of the car and stared at the place feeling useless. Then I heard some yelling out back and knew I had to help. I moved without thinking around the house, using the side opposite the one taken by Aunt Mae and Sheriff Morrison.

I peeked around the corner of the house and took in the terrifying sight. A tall man I'd never seen before was holding a gun to Amber's back. He must have hit her earlier because her eye was swollen and she seemed groggy. The Sheriff, Deputy Wise, and Aunt Mae were taking what little cover they could find and held their weapons at their sides, carefully pointing the guns at the ground, ready if needed. Elias was there too and he whimpered, "Why are you doing this?"

Robert answered, "It's best if you just keep quiet Elias." Then he addressed the tall stranger. "Dominic, we've been partners for years. Why are you doing this?"

The stranger snarled at Robert, "If you hadn't been so greedy and just given me what I asked for, this wouldn't have happened."

Robert shot back, anger in his voice, "If you had just done your job and gone back to Atlanta with the payment agreed to, everything would have been fine. But no, you were the one to get greedy. You had to have more."

The gunman barked again at Robert. "There was more money involved than you told me. You lied to me. I'm done being lied to by you and always being on the short end. Always having to hide and do the dirty work" Dominic looked over at the deputies and Sheriff Morrison. "You get them to leave or I will kill her."

Robert's face drooped and went white. "Please, don't hurt her. We've known each other for a long time and Amber is innocent. Let her go. If we get out of this, I'll give you whatever you want."

Sheriff Morrison yelled, "This is the police. Lower your weapon. We have you surrounded and there's no escape. It's best if you just lower the gun and surrender."

Dominic shouted back, "I don't think so. I have two hostages and you'll do what I tell you. I'm in charge here."

And right after the gunman finished speaking, Gypsy picked the worst possible time to find me and look for attention. She meowed, numerous times and loudly. Everyone heard the cat mewing and looked in my direction. The stranger brandishing the gun included.

Dominic was now aware that someone might be sneaking up on him from his blind side and that caused him to make a mistake. He tugged on Amber and took a single step backwards towards the safety of the house. But there were two cats playing with a leaf behind him and they decided now was a good time to sharpen their claws on his pants leg. He tripped over them with Amber crashing down on top of him, losing his gun in the process.

And that was the cue for Deputy Wise and Sheriff Morrison to rush the scene. Robert also acted and he kicked the gun away from Dominic and Amber. Robert then jumped on top of his partner and pinned him to the ground. But just moments later, the Sheriff and Deputy Wise piled onto Robert and Dominic. The officers tried to pin them both to the ground, however Dominic had other ideas.

He must have been strong because Dominic flung Deputy Wise off him easily. After that he sprung to his feet and sprinted off for the trees just beyond the back yard. But as he approached the tree line, Guardrail appeared from behind a large trunk and held out one of his meaty arms. The arm caught the fleeing man in the neck and clothes lined him, causing him to come off his feet and fall hard on his back. The process left Dominic disabled, on the ground, and gasping for air.

The Sheriff made Robert lay on the ground, face down and cuffed him. Deputy Wise sprinted over to the now gasping Dominic and quickly put the cuffs on him, giving Guardrail a quick side glance as a kind of thanks-for-the-help gesture.

Aunt Mae ran over to attend to Elias and Amber. She escorted the two over to the back steps and helped them to sit and take a moment to calm down.

Sheriff Morrison read Robert his rights then helped

him to his feet. Robert couldn't help himself and blurted out, "You must be a lucky man. There is no way a small town, know-nothing police department could figure something like this out."

The Sheriff shoved Robert in the direction of the cruiser out front. "Humble to the end I see. Well, tell it to your lawyer. I don't care." Sheriff Morrison and Deputy Wise then carted both of the bound men to the police car and I followed at a distance.

Edith and Lily came sauntering across a side yard towards the cruiser yelling 'Shoo' at the cats the whole way. I met them on the front lawn not far from the cruiser and Edith asked, "Deary, what happened? We saw Robert and a stranger being put in the police car."

I shrugged, "To be honest, I'm not completely sure. Weren't you supposed to be directing traffic?"

Lily snorted. "Guardrail thinks he's the big boss of the world. When there was no traffic for him to lord over, he quit and left the detour business to us so he could go see what he might do to help the police."

"I guess you ladies did a good job. The road is still empty." I scanned Main Street as I spoke.

Edith jumped in, pointing her wrinkled finger down the road. "The strip on Main Street back there is closed for the fair. Everyone is using River Road today anyway, so we didn't have much to do."

I smiled, "Small town life does have some benefits."

At that point, the Sheriff came back over to me and was scowling. "After this all settles down, we need to have a talk missy."

"Anytime. But is it going to really be a talk, or a scolding?"

He looked at me fatherly, through the brim of his hat. "A little of both, but first I need to pin down all the details of what happened here. And against all of my warnings, you still somehow managed to inject yourself into this. Which means I now have to debrief you."

"I'll help anyway I can. It's what we do in Potter's Mill."

"I guess it is. But I can't stress this point enough, not if it puts you in danger or interferes with police business. Remember that next time, please." The Sheriff smiled, just a little. Then the smile disappeared and he turned to scowl at Guardrail. "If you ever mess with official police work again, I *will* arrest you."

Guardrail made his best attempt to look innocent. "Who me? I was just stretching out. The dude ran into my arm. I stayed behind the tree and out of the way like you asked."

"Don't get smart with me." The Sheriff eyed him

for a moment, then added, "But thanks, I wasn't in the mood for a foot chase."

Dog Breath had appeared, seemingly from nowhere, and added, "I don't usually worry about Guardrail being smart myself." The Sheriff silenced Dog with a single look.

Aunt Mae made her way over to us with Amber and Elias in tow. Elias was helping Amber walk and she now held a bag of frozen peas to her swollen eye. My aunt asked me, "Are you alright? I told you to stay in the car."

"I know. But there was so much shouting and commotion." I paused. "You know, I can honestly tell you I learned that I'm not as brave as I thought. And you showed me that there is training and skill involved in dealing with dangerous suspects and situations."

"Wow. That actually, maybe coulda might sound like you did learn something. Bread me and fry me in batter." She smiled, just a little, and I was glad to see the Aunt Mae I knew once again. It was then I discerned how stressful this murder investigation actually was for Aunt Mae and the Sheriff.

Mae smiled at me and asked, "Can you wait with Amber and Elias? I called for an ambulance to attend to her injuries." She then headed over to the cruiser to finish her official business.

I put my arm around Amber to hold her and offer

comfort. She was crying and I knew it wasn't because of the injuries suffered from the blow to her head. I offered, "You poor thing. Mae called for an ambulance. We'll get you looked at and patched up like new."

"My eye is fine. It'll heal. It's my heart that is aching. How could he do such a terrible thing?" Amber sniffled while she talked.

I looked at her a second. "I have no idea how to answer that, Amber. But you're my friend and I am here to help you. With anything you need."

"Why? No one cares about me."

"You showed me kindness when I came out here to talk to you, even though you didn't have to. You trusted me like a true small town local. And we take care of our own. No one should have to endure something like this alone and I want to help one of my friends."

"Wow. I haven't had a friend in a long time. Isn't that pathetic?" She wiped some tears from her eyes.

I smiled back at her. "Well, to be honest, that is kind of sad. But your friend drought is over and you now have more friends then you know. We'll help you get through this with anything you need."

She sobbed a little and squeezed my hand on her shoulder. "Thanks. But the first thing I need to do is understand how my father could do something this awful. And what am I going to do without him?"

I had no real answer but tried. "That may take you some time to figure out. But don't worry about that, you're strong and smart and will get through it."

Elias, who had been uncharacteristically quiet, spoke. "You can stay here as long as necessary, Amber." We both looked back at him like we were seeing the grumpy chicken itself.

I regained control and closed my mouth that hung open in astonishment. "Thanks." I meant to say more to him, but it's all that came out. At that point, the ambulance arrived and I helped them get in. Then the paramedics took Elias and Amber to the medical center in the next town over.

I stood on the lawn with a sense of relief mixed with dismay. The murder was solved, sure, but I was starting to see just how much Elias and Amber would need us now. Their lives would never be the same. I had no idea what would be necessary, but promised myself that we would be there for them.

Mae came back over to me as the Sheriff and Deputy Wise drove off in the cruiser with the prisoners. She said, "I need to get back to the station and file reports. Kelly asked me to bring his car back for him. We need to get another cruiser for this town. It's not right how much we use Kelly's own car. Hey, sweetie, you want a ride home before I go back to the station? "

"No. I think I can use a nice long walk about now. To clear my head."

She smiled at me. "It's overwhelming, isn't it?" She saw the confusion on my face, so Aunt Mae continued. "The mix of feelings. I've solved a few crimes in my years. And it is always surprising how emotions still swirl inside me afterwards."

I sighed. "I had no idea how overwhelming and exhausting solving crime is until now."

"Well said, honey. Now don't ever forget that and stick to the pub business!" She hugged me tight.

I spoke into her shoulder. "I don't know. I think I did pretty good?"

"Don't even tease me about it. I don't want you messing with police business ever again. It's too dangerous."

"Hmm. Where have I heard that before?"

"Don't sass me. I'm your loving Aunt, but I can still tan your hide if you get out of line."

"I don't doubt that for a moment, Auntie. I saw you in action today. But, like I said earlier, I learned a lot going through all of this. I just want to get back to my business, worrying about normal stuff."

Mae chuckled, "I've been to The Grumpy Chicken. remember? I *know* there is nothing normal about that place."

"It is to me. I am understanding that more every day!" I smiled and, for the first time in days, I felt a hint of happiness.

Chapter Nineteen

The pub was full to capacity and the atmosphere was happy for the first time in days, almost celebratory with news of an arrest in the Holland murder investigation. Everyone seemed to have their own story of how they helped figure it out or capture the suspects. But I knew most were fabricated tall tales since I found the body and witnessed the take down of the culprits.

I sat at a table with Aunt Mae and the Sheriff and we enjoyed a cold beer together. I asked the Sheriff, "So how much trouble am I in?"

The Sheriff sat up straight and his voice got a little deeper. "We'll talk about that later. But let's just say you're lucky that plane ticket tip was spot on. We almost let him slip out of the country."

Mae added, "Yeah, but we couldn't arrest him right off because he had an alibi for the time of the murder. He was seen by multiple people all over town and he had receipts that checked out on his credit cards. It all seems obvious now that we know he didn't actually choke her to death. But he certainly made the arrangements to have his partner do it for him. And all over some money."

The Sheriff eyed Mae and said, "We should have held Robert and never released him. I know we discussed it and did the right thing letting him go home that night since we had no hard evidence. But both of us knew there was something off about him."

Mae replied, "I know, but we had no idea he had a partner. And poor Amber. She was so worried about Donna, 'The Black Widow,' killing her father. Only now she has to deal with the fact her father had Donna murdered for inheritance. It's so bizarre, and sad for Amber."

She was right on all accounts, but it was a downer. I tried to end the self wallowing. "Well it all worked out and you got your man."

Sheriff Morrison produced a rare smile. "Yeah we did. And thanks for your help. But if you do it again ..."

I rose holding my palm at him to stop. "I know. I know. Make sure to use your small cuffs when you arrest me, I have small wrists." I smiled at him. "I need to get back to work. See ya around." I said goodbye and rose to make the rounds.

I spotted Dog talking breathlessly. I couldn't hear him very well, but I was sure he was bragging. As hard as it is for me to believe, Dog Breath was telling, and retelling, one of his gonzo stories that was actually true. I had to give it to him, Dog threw out the idea of a hit man early. And pigs must be flying now because it turned out he was, technically, right.

Robert orchestrated the crime and the actual murderer was paid by him to commit the deed. We argued about whether Dominic, Robert's partner, was a real hit man. And the Sheriff was consulted to settle the argument. He even looked up the definition of hit man in an online dictionary. Sheriff Morrison then concluded that even though Dominic was Robert's long time partner, he acted as a hit man.

I saw Digger approach Dog and slip him some money. Digger snapped at him, "I still say this isn't right because there were two definitions. According to the first definition, he should've worked for a crime syndicate, and he didn't. The second definition the Sheriff used was too vague. He wasn't a real hit man. It was just his partner." Digger was tight with his money so I am sure it hurt to pay Dog on what seemed like a sure bet.

On seeing the pay off, I interjected, "Boys, not in the dining room, please. Gambling could shut me down." I moved on to let them stew in their argument, which I knew would continue.

I felt happy like everyone else and the nervous energy I carried over the last few days was gone. I located Dixie and said, "Hey, I think it's appropriate to offer a special to sell off the rest of the huckleberry liquors. What do ya think?"

Dixie winked at me. I guess that was her new thing

now. She said, "Specials would be good. I usually get better tips when the drinks are on sale. Oh!" Dixie lowered her voice and leaned in close. "I also had some requests from our regulars for Gator's special peach pie. I told them to talk to you later.

"OK, but not in the dining room, of course. I keep saying I'm going to stop selling that firewater under the table, but everyone likes it so much and the money is just too good."

Dixie chuckled, "You don't have to tell me. And I like the stuff, too. Come to think of it, I think I've seen you drink it as well."

"Sometimes." I was watching everyone enjoying the fun when Beth approached, looking for gossip I'm sure. I greeted her, "What's new down at the community center?"

Beth made an odd grunt through her nose then said, "Same as always, organizing people and events is difficult work. But I'm up to the task."

I forced a smile. "I'm sure you are."

Beth continued, "Thanks. We never spoke again, I was so hoping we would."

"Well, the murder is solved now and everybody knows what happened. I was so busy the last couple of days. I'm sorry, I wasn't ignoring you."

"I certainly hope not. But I know you were in the center of this thing and I would still like to hear everything."

"When I have a few minutes. Sure Beth. But today it's real busy here at the Chicken and it's not a good time."

Piper came to my rescue. She had a drink in her hand and grabbed my elbow. She whispered, "Ida has some things to show you in the office."

I finished my conversation with Beth by adding, "I'll have Dixie make you some sweet. I need to get into the kitchen right now. But I'll talk with you later."

Beth added, "Thanks, and I am going to hold you to that!"

I left Beth and headed for the office with Piper. Ida was still at the laptops when we arrived, working furiously while eating one of the free sandwiches she felt was due her. She looked up when she saw us and began talking. "You should see this. It's so interesting. Robert did business with all the wrong kinds of people in Atlanta. And he hid it well. But he's been in debt for a long time, and he owed the wrong people. It was a miracle that no one else got hurt after the murder. This dude Robert has been partners with for years is bad news and had a real long record. I can't believe we had someone as dangerous as this Dominic hiding in our little town."

I raised my eyebrows. "Why? Elias was dealing with loans from the mob, and he hid that. So Robert dealing with gangsters from Atlanta doesn't surprise me that much, I guess. But I wonder if Donna or Amber knew of anything?"

Piper answered, "From what I hear Amber is devastated. She had no clue, or so it seems."

I turned to Piper standing behind me and said, "I heard that too. I'm actually planning on going out there to bring her and Elias some food later. They're both pretty shaken up by all this."

Ida added, "What the heck was going on in that house? I'll never look at the Holland place the same way."

"I guess none of us will." I sat on the edge of my desk, well it was more like Ida's desk now. Thinking how strange all of this was. I asked, "Why are you still set up here? To chase leads for a solved crime?"

She shrugged. "Nope. Just tying up loose ends."

I scrunched up my face. "Can't you do that at home?"

"Sure. But it's more fun here."

I gave her the side eye. "This is my office, not a hack shack."

Piper laughed at the conversation and then Ida's tone changed as she chided me, "Hey, don't you ever check your email? Your inbox is over flowing. And what's this? You father is coming home. He should be here soon. Said he couldn't get you on your cell phone."

"Yeah, I lost it somewhere during the chase the other day. Wait, my dad is coming home – like soon as in today?"

"Yep, and he says he has a surprise for you."

"Well, that makes two surprises. Because the first surprise was what in the blazes are you doing in my email?"

Piper chuckled, "I think it's safe to assume she checks everyone's email. Seems to be her best source of information." Piper then picked up a copy of her latest issue of The Potter's Mill Oracle. "Here, have a read. I wrote one of my best stories ever, if I do say so myself. You feature prominently in some parts."

Bones burst into the office and bellowed, "You got to hide me! Abbey is here! And so is my girlfriend."

I shrugged, "Who's Abbey?"

Bones bobbed his head at me. "You know, the clerk from town hall I made a date with."

"You're on your own, Bones. If you can't control your hormones, you got to clean up the mess on your own."

I felt Dog's presence more than I saw him. His voice confirmed he was just outside the office.

"Hey, who erased the stuff on the whiteboard?"

Bones answered, "It just went away on it's own yesterday, right about the time of the big arrest."

Dog stroked his long gray pony tail a couple of times. "Are you messing with me? How can it just disappear all on its own? This is bad. Going to cost me money. I was all set to win a bet when I showed Patrick Cummings that writing. This would be kinda of funny if it wasn't happening to me."

I laughed, "You're right Dog. It's funny to me and I told you not to be betting in the pub. Serves you right."

"You're all just jealous because I was right about the hit man!" Dog Breath turned and left to go drink some more beer at the bar.

I stood and said, "Well, I better get out front to help Dixie and check on things. With Dog's head all swollen with being 'right,' the boys have been acting like The Three Stooges."

Ida added, "Don't let them hear that. They'll be betting and arguing over which one is Larry for days." She paused and looked up realizing we were staring at her. "Larry was the funny one, right?"

Piper laughed out loud and couldn't hold her tongue, "OMG! Ida, I would leave The Three Stooges humor alone. There has got to be some ancient curse that condemns women to live with men who think the stooges are funny. I, and every other woman, will never understand it."

I left chuckling and made my way out front and went behind the bar. Something strange was happening down at one end, and not surprisingly, it was the end of the bar that Dog Breath, Digger, and Guardrail called home. Guardrail was kneeling curiously on his stool, which made me nervous because the big man now hovered much too high over my bar. A man his size should not use a stool like that and it's a miracle he didn't tip over. Animated and waving his hands, he implored, "I saw it, right there. It was a mouse, well more than one. But it's weird. Almost like I could see through them like ghosts."

Digger was sitting on his stool, holding his stomach and laughing about as hard as I've seen. He said through his tears of glee, "That may be, but why did you have to climb up on your stool and make that weird sound?"

Dog whined, "I can't believe I just missed that sound he makes. And while I was finding out I lost my money with Patrick."

I added, "Guardrail, I've paid for the best extermination methods available in Potter's Mill. I'm sure we don't have mice in here. And the cats around the building finish off any that may be stupid enough to slip through the cracks. Now sit on your stool, properly."

Guardrail complied with my request but he insisted, "I'm telling ya, there was more than one and I could see through them. Like they weren't real."

I was spared from more disturbing images of a cowering Guardrail when the front door opened to reveal my father. He had been out of town getting medical attention for a bad cough and the treatment must have had an effect. He sported a large smile and stood straighter than usual. I could swear his hair looked fuller, and a little less gray. He used large strides to move his large frame through the dining room and came over to give me a hug. I was glad he was back and it made me feel like things were truly getting back to normal. I saw the boys at the end of the bar were gawking as we hugged. My father was not known as a warm man and this was not the vision conjured up with the mention of his name. Dad said, "I'm so happy to be back at the Chicken. We had a real whodunit going on for a while I hear."

"I guess you could say that."

"I am saying it. Are you all right? I was so worried about you. You know, finding the body."

"I'm fine, Dad. Just a little tired."

Dad scanned me head to toe. "Well, I'm glad to hear you're fine. You look good. And I got a surprise for you. Some very special people are coming to visit us. But that's all I'm saying for now.

I'm going to let them tell you all about themselves when they get here tomorrow. You'll just have to trust me, it's better that way. And it'll be fun, I promise."

"That's … that's kind of strange. But okay I guess."

"You'll love it. Trust me."

"Ginger!" Bessie Houston had to raise her voice to be heard over all the background noise. I almost didn't recognize it when I heard it.

I spun to see her with full hands as usual. "Bessie. Nice to see you. We're rescheduled for tomorrow, or did I get my wires crossed?"

"No, I wanted to come by now to join the party for a little while. Right now, this is the place to be in Potter's Mill." Bessie nodded to my father and said, "Well, if it isn't Thomas O'Mallory in the flesh. Welcome home, and I hope you're feeling better."

My dad coughed a little then snapped back, "Don't call me Thomas, you know I hate that. Call me Tom."

Bessie laughed, "Gruff and to the point. Wouldn't expect anything else. A lot has happened since you were gone."

"I heard." My father then eyed what was in her hands. "What's that?"

Bessie answered, "A gift for Ginger. She was so sweet, rescheduling craft night and working so hard with the police." She handed me the large, heavy box with a big bow on top.

Tom said, "You mean reschedule Stitch N Bitch?"

Bessie cringed. "I'll make you a deal, Tom. I'll call you Tom if you don't call craft night that name."

Tom huffed and said, "Done. Now let's drink on it." And he waved a hand in the air like he was addressing an adoring Roman crowd, spun, and went to have a drink with the boys.

I turned to Bessie. "Sorry about him. He's not himself today. He's just happy to be home. And you shouldn't have. Thank you."

She pointed at the box. "You're more than welcome. Go ahead open it."

"And I'm glad we're on for tomorrow. I ordered more wings and it should be well attended after the week we've had – plus it's Friday night." I spoke as I took the lid off the box. "Holy cow, this is a big one."

Bessie beamed. "It's an apothecary jar for the pickled eggs. I know you had the others broken. This one is big, but the manufacturer says it's made with glass so strong and thick, it's unbreakable."

I laughed. "Guardrail will be happy. But this thing is so big I don't think I can afford the amount of eggs it will take to fill it."

Bessie pointed out, "Who says you have to fill it."

A booming voice cut through the sound filled dining room like a fighter jet flashing through a wispy cloud. It was Guardrail's happy voice. "Is that a new pickled egg jar?"

Guardrail came rushing over through the crowd. Edith and Lily saw him and knew something was happening. So they decided to join in and came over too. Guardrail bubbled and put his arm around Edith. He dwarfed her and said, "And how are the best biker chicks in town."

Edith and Lily giggled like high school teens at his comment. Edith asked, "When are we going for a ride again?"

Guardrail shrugged and continued. "I don't know. Not tonight for sure. We're celebrating and I've had too much to drink."

Lily added, "Is that a new pickled egg jar? It's so pretty."

I nodded. "Yes it is. A gift from Bessie Houston."

Lily poked Edith and said, "You know, we should pay to fill the jar the first time for Guardrail. To thank him for the fun ride on the hogs. He loves those eggs so much."

Guardrail shivered his big body and said, "No.

That's okay. And please stop calling my bike a hog; it's just not right. You know what, I'm the one that eats all the eggs anyway. I'll pay to fill it, in honor of Potter's Gang getting to the bottom of the Holland murder."

Lily objected, "No! We don't have a name, do we?"

Dog Breath was just behind Guardrail and added, "I thought we agreed to the Grumpy Gumshoes?"

In unison, everyone screamed, "No!"

I smiled at the bedlam. It was normal small town mayhem and I couldn't be happier to deal with it.

Catalog of Books

Thanks for reading! I hope you enjoyed the book and it would mean so much to me if you could leave a review. Reviews help authors gain more exposure and keep us writing your favorite stories.

You can find all of my books by visiting my Author Page.

Sign up for Constance Barker's New Releases Newsletter where you can find out when my next book is coming out and for special discounted pricing.

I never share or sell your email.

Visit me on Facebook and give me feedback on the characters and their stories.

Old School Diner Cozy Mysteries

Murder at Stake

Murder Well Done

A Side Order of Deception

Murder, Basted and Barbecued

The Curiosity Shop Cozy Mysteries

The Curious Case of the Cursed Spectacles

The Curious Case of the Cursed Dice

The Curious Case of the Cursed Dagger

The Curious Case of the Cursed Looking Glass

The We're Not Dead Yet Club

Fetch a Pail of Murder

Wedding Bells and Death Knells

Murder or Bust

Pinched, Pilfered and a Pitchfork

A Hot Spot of Murder

Witchy Women of Coven Grove Series

The Witching on the Wall

A Witching Well of Magic

Witching the Night Away

Witching There's Another Way

Witching Your Life Away

Witching You Wouldn't Go

Witching for a Miracle

Teasen & Pleasen Hair Salon Series

A Hair Raising Blowout

Wash, Rinse, Die

Holiday Hooligans

Color Me Dead

False Nails & Tall Tales

Caesar's Creek Series

A Frozen Scoop of Murder (Caesars Creek Mystery Series Book One)

Death by Chocolate Sundae (Caesars Creek Mystery Series Book Two)

Soft Serve Secrets (Caesars Creek Mystery Series Book Three)

Ice Cream You Scream (Caesars Creek Mystery Series Book Four)

Double Dip Dilemma (Caesars Creek Mystery Series Book Five)

Melted Memories (Caesars Creek Mystery Series Book Six)

Triple Dip Debacle(Caesars Creek Mystery Series Book Seven)

Whipped Wedding Woes(Caesars Creek Mystery Series Book Eight)

A Sprinkle of Tropical Trouble(Caesars Creek Mystery Series Book Nine)

A Drizzle of Deception(Caesars Creek Mystery Series Book Ten)

Sweet Home Mystery Series

Creamed at the Coffee Cabana (Sweet Home Mystery Series Book One)

A Caffeinated Crunch (Sweet Home Mystery Series Book Two)

A Frothy Fiasco (Sweet Home Mystery Series Book Three)

Punked by the Pumpkin(Sweet Home Mystery Series Book Four)

Peppermint Pandemonium(Sweet Home Mystery Series Book Five)

Expresso Messo(Sweet Home Mystery Series Book Six)

A Cuppa Cruise Conundrum(Sweet Home Mystery Series Book Seven)

The Brewing Bride(Sweet Home Mystery Series Book Eight)

Whispering Pines Mystery Series

A Sinister Slice of Murder

Sanctum of Shadows (Whispering Pines Mystery Series)

Curse of the Bloodstone Arrow (Whispering Pines Mystery Series)

Fright Night at the Haunted Inn (Whispering Pines Mystery Series)